"Maybe...n
when you j
heart,

Eric looked down at her, his eyes serious. "I haven't been willing to do that for a long time," he admitted.

She searched his eyes, wanting to ask the question that hovered on her lips, but afraid to do so. Yet he seemed to read her mind, and answered it.

"I've felt differently about a lot of things since I met you, Kate," he told her quietly.

"So...so have I," she confessed. "But I'm still not sure what to do. I've been praying for guidance."

He smiled and squeezed her hand. "Since I've been doing the same thing, why don't we leave it in the Lord's hands for the moment? He'll show us the way in His own time."

She nodded. "I think that's a good plan.... But I hope He doesn't wait too long," she added impulsively.

Eric chuckled. "You and me *both*."

Books by Irene Hannon

Love Inspired

*Home for the Holidays #6
*A Groom of Her Own #16
*A Family to Call Her Own #25
It Had to Be You #58
One Special Christmas #77

*Vows

IRENE HANNON

has been a writer for as long as she can remember. This prolific author of romance novels for both the inspirational and traditional markets began her career at age ten, when she won a story contest conducted by a national children's magazine. Today, in addition to penning her heartwarming stories of love and faith, Irene keeps quite busy with her "day job" in corporate communications. In her "spare" time, she enjoys performing in community musical theater productions. The author and her husband, Tom—whom she describes as "my own romantic hero"—make their home in St. Louis, Missouri.

One Special Christmas
Irene Hannon

Published by Steeple Hill Books™

STEEPLE HILL BOOKS

Steeple
Hill™

ISBN 0-373-87077-9

ONE SPECIAL CHRISTMAS

For I know well the plans I have in mind for you,
says the Lord, plans for your welfare not for woe,
plans to give you a future full of hope.

—*Jeremiah* 29:11

To my brother, Jim,
and his lovely bride, Teresa—
May all your happily-ever-after dreams come true.

Prologue

It was over in moments, yet it seemed to happen in slow motion.

The car swerved suddenly, fishtailed wildly as the driver struggled for control on the icy road. Then it skidded sideways off the steep shoulder, rolling over once before coming to rest, upright, at the bottom of the embankment.

Eric Carlson watched in horror, his hands tightening instinctively on the wheel as the accident unfolded a few hundred feet in front of him. Though he didn't doubt his eyes, the terrible scene had an odd air of unreality about it, seeming to happen in utter quiet, like an old silent movie. The sleet hitting his car roof, combined with the volume of the radio that Cindy had just cranked up, must have masked the grating sound of metal being crushed, the high-pitched crackle of shattering glass—and the inevitable screams that would accompany such a traumatic crash. But Eric could imagine them, and he swallowed convulsively as his breath lodged in his throat.

Dear God, he prayed as the full impact of what he'd just witnessed slammed home. He slowed his car as quickly as the icy road would allow and eased it over to the shoulder.

"What are you doing?" Cindy demanded stridently.

He set the brake and reached into the back for his bag. "Exactly what you think I'm doing," he replied tersely.

"Oh, for heaven's sake, Eric, we're going to be late for the party! They're serving dinner at eight. Let's just call 911 and get out of here. Those other Good Samaritans can help," she said impatiently, gesturing toward two other cars that had also stopped.

He turned to his wife, and as he looked at her petulant expression he wondered what had drawn him to her a dozen years ago. Her blond beauty had attracted him, certainly. And he'd been flattered that someone so sophisticated had found him appealing. But surely there had been more. Hadn't her heart once been kind and caring? Hadn't the smiles she'd given him in those early days been tender and warm? Or had he seen only what he'd wanted to see, imagined what had never been there at all?

As the years had passed and the chasm between them had widened, he'd been forced to admit that perhaps it was his perception—not Cindy—that had changed. Or perhaps she had simply become more of what she had always been as she grew disillusioned with him and disenchanted with the demands of his profession—the "doctor stuff," as she demeaningly termed it. He was well aware that his dedication to his work grated on her, that she felt his devotion to his patients diminished his devotion to her. And perhaps it did. Perhaps if he had been able to give her the kind of attention she needed, their relationship wouldn't be disintegrating. Yet how could he give anything less than one hundred percent to his profession? It was a dilemma he wrestled with constantly, but always the answers eluded him. All he knew was that both of them were unhappy in their marriage.

But it was too late now to alter their status, Eric reminded himself grimly. He had meant the vows they'd made on their wedding day, including "For better, for worse." After all, as his old maiden aunt used to say, he and Cindy had made their bed. Now they had to lie in it.

Eric knew they couldn't go on like this. But his repeated suggestions that they seek counseling were always met with cold sarcasm—and a cold shoulder. As he looked at her now, in the shadowy light of the car, she seemed almost like a stranger.

Cindy shifted uncomfortably under her husband's scrutiny, and when she spoke again her tone was more conciliatory. "Look, those other people will do whatever they can until help arrives, Eric. They don't need you."

"I'm a doctor, Cindy."

"You're a pediatrician."

She didn't say "just," but the implication was there in her disparaging tone. A muscle in his jaw clenched as he handed her the cell phone. "Call 911." Then he stepped out into the darkness, turning up his collar as he strode toward the embankment, sleet stinging his face much as the familiar gibe always stung his heart.

By the time he made it down to the smashed car, slipping and sliding all the way, the other two motorists were already there. Both had flashlights and were peering into the vehicle. They glanced up when Eric approached.

"How many inside?" he asked.

"Looks like just two. A man and a woman," one replied. He eyed Eric's bag. "Are you a doctor?"

"Yes."

"Well, the woman's conscious but the man doesn't look too good," the other passerby reported dubiously.

Eric strode around to the passenger's side of the car, and with some effort the three of them were able to force open the jammed door.

"One of you give me some light," he instructed as he leaned down to look in, noting with relief that the woman's seat belt was securely in place. He touched her shoulder gently, and she turned to him, her eyes wide and dazed.

For just a moment, Eric simply stared at her. Even in the harsh beam of the flashlight, she had the face of a Madonna—a perfect oval, with dark hair and even darker eyes. She was like something out of a Raphael painting, he thought numbly, momentarily taken aback by her beauty. Her looks were classic, timeless—and marred by a nasty bump that was rising rapidly on her left temple. Abruptly he shifted his focus from her physical attributes to her physical condition.

"I'm a doctor. Can you hear me?" He spoke slowly, enunciating each word carefully.

She nodded jerkily. "I—I'm all right. Please... please take care of my husband," she pleaded.

He looked past her, noting the unnatural position of

the male driver, who lay crumpled behind the steering wheel, as well as the blood seeping from the corner of his mouth. "All right. Try not to move. An ambulance is on the way."

"Can I do anything to help?" the flashlight holder asked as Eric straightened.

"The two of you can give me some light on the other side," he said over his shoulder. The other motorist had managed to get the driver's door open, and the two men focused the beams of their lights on the injured man as Eric bent down to examine him.

He wasn't wearing a seat belt, Eric noted. Right off the bat, that was a major strike against him. And the car was an older-model compact, without air bags. Strike two. Eric felt for the man's pulse. Shallow. And his respiration was uneven. He showed signs of major trauma, including head-and-neck injuries—which meant possible spinal damage, Eric noted after a quick visual scan.

Frowning, he glanced up and his gaze met that of the woman passenger. She stared at him, and he saw the fear in her eyes suddenly mushroom at his grim expression.

"He's going to be all right, isn't he?" she pleaded desperately, the stricken look on her face making his gut twist painfully. "This can't be happening! Not tonight! Not now!" She let out a strangled sob and turned her attention to her husband, reaching over to touch his face. "You'll be all right, Jack. I know you will. You have to be!" she said fiercely.

The man's breathing suddenly grew more erratic, and Eric snapped open his bag and deftly withdrew his stethoscope. As he listened to the man's fading pulse, his own heart ratcheted into double time. *God, please let the paramedics arrive soon!* he prayed.

But within seconds it became clear that they weren't going to arrive soon enough. The man's breathing grew more labored with each breath, and obviously he was fighting a losing battle to suck air into his lungs. Eric reached for his bag again. In all his years of medical training, in all his years of trauma work, he'd never had to open an airway in the field, let alone with makeshift lighting and icy sleet pricking the back of his neck. But as the seconds ticked by, it was obvious that if he didn't, this man was going to die. He couldn't let that happen—especially after seeing the anguished look in the woman's eyes.

Eric drew in a steadying breath. Then, without further hesitation, he deftly performed the procedure, aware of, but steeling himself against, the woman's startled gasp. Only when he'd finished did he glance up, noting with alarm the pallor of her face and the glazed look in her eyes. She was starting to turn shocky, Eric realized. And he couldn't handle two trauma cases at once.

Just as he began to panic, the welcome sound of approaching sirens pierced the night air. He closed his eyes and slowly he let out his breath as relief washed over him. Thank God! He needed all the help he could get—and the sooner the better.

Within moments the paramedics joined him, and he explained the situation in clipped phrases, the economy of his language honed during years of emergency-room work where every second counted. As one paramedic temporarily distracted the woman, he spoke softly to the other two.

"Probable severe neck-and-head trauma. I opened an airway, but he's still very unstable. Handle him with kid gloves."

"No problem. We've worked cases like this before," one of them assured him.

"Do you need me to stay and help?"

"We've got it covered. But thanks for stopping. Immediate medical attention can make all the difference, as you know."

Eric nodded, then straightened. He spoke briefly to the policeman on the scene, then made his way up the embankment.

As he crested the rise and stepped onto the pavement, he glanced back once more toward the accident scene, surrealistically illuminated by the police-car headlights and the rotating red-and-white beacon on the ambulance. The woman was standing now, her arms wrapped tightly around her, and though it was clear the paramedic was urging her to sit in one of the vehicles, she was adamantly shaking her head. Her gaze was locked on the two men who were carefully extricating her husband from the battered car. Eric could feel her panic, could sense her almost-palpable fear even from this distance.

Would Cindy look like that if something ever happened to him? he wondered. But even before the question formed, he knew the disheartening answer. Any love they had once shared had died long ago.

For just a moment, despite the man's severe injuries, Eric almost envied him. His wife's deep, abiding love was evident in her eyes, her expression, her very body language. Her husband was obviously the center of her world. And Eric knew intuitively that she was the cen-

ter of his. Which was as it should be in a good marriage.

Finally, unable to look at the heartrending scene any
longer, he turned away, his gut twisting painfully. He
was reasonably certain he'd saved the man's life. But
as he reached his car and slipped back inside, he wondered for just a moment if he'd done anyone a favor.
Eric suspected that the road ahead would not be an easy
one—for either him or his wife. That tonight was only
the beginning of their trauma.

Maybe Cindy had been right, after all. Maybe he just
should have driven on.

Chapter One

Five years later

"Mrs. Nolan, the doctor will see Sarah now."

Kate glanced up from the book she was reading to her daughter and smiled. "All right. Thanks." She slung her purse over her shoulder and stood, reaching down to take Sarah's hand. "Come on, honey. It's time to go in."

"Do I have to?"

Kate gazed down into the large, dark eyes—a mirror image of her own—and with an apologetic glance at the nurse, sat back down. She pulled Sarah close and spoke gently. "You don't want to have those nasty tummyaches anymore, do you, honey? The doctor can help make them go away. And I'll stay with you the whole time. I promise."

Sarah's eyes welled with tears and she sniffed. "I don't like doctors."

"You used to like Dr. Davis, remember? And this doctor is a friend of his. So I'm sure you'll like him, too."

"He's not going to give me a shot, is he?"

"I don't think so. Not today."

Sarah's lower lip quivered. "Promise you'll stay with me?" she pleaded tremulously.

"Of course I will, honey."

She gave her daughter a quick, reassuring hug and stood again, her heart contracting as Sarah's small, trusting hand reached for hers. She couldn't even bear the thought that something serious might be wrong with her. Sarah was the only thing that gave her life any meaning or joy. Though she'd tried not to worry during the past week as she'd waited for this appointment, she'd met with little success. Nights were the worst. She kept waking up in a cold sweat as increasingly frightening scenarios played themselves out in her dreams. Sarah was all she had now, and she would do anything—anything—to keep her well and safe and happy.

She tightened her grip encouragingly and smiled down at her daughter, trying futilely to control the almost painful thumping of her heart as they followed the nurse inside. Everything would turn out fine, she told herself resolutely. It had to. Except she knew from experience that that was a lie. Everything didn't *have* to turn out fine. There were lots of times when it didn't—no matter how hard you wished for it or wanted it or prayed for it.

The nurse stopped at the door of an examining room and ushered them inside.

"The doctor will be with you in just a few minutes," she promised.

"Shall I undress Sarah?" Kate asked.

The woman glanced at Sarah's shorts and crop top, noted how tenaciously the little girl clung to her mother, and smiled as she shook her head. "I don't think so. The doctor should be able to check everything out just like that. If not, he'll let you know."

Kate watched the woman leave, then forced her lips into what she hoped was a cheery smile. "Shall we finish our story?" She held up the book she'd brought with her from the waiting room.

Sarah nodded, and as Kate sat down the youngster climbed onto her lap. Though her daughter quickly became engrossed in the story, Kate couldn't so easily forget where they were. Or why. Even when Sarah got the sniffles she worried excessively, and this mysterious ache in her daughter's stomach was making Kate's own stomach clench painfully.

When a brief knock interrupted her reading a few minutes later, she jerked involuntarily, then glanced up with a troubled gaze as the door swung open.

Eric stopped abruptly on the threshold as he stared at the woman whose face had been indelibly etched into his mind on that cold, tragic evening five years before. It was a night memorable in many ways—none of them pleasant. It had begun with the terrible accident, and had ended with his wife's announcement that she wanted a divorce. For years he'd tried to put the events of that dismal evening behind him. But the one thing he'd never been able to forget was this woman's stunning face and the desperate love he'd seen reflected in her expressive eyes.

Her face was still stunning, he noted. But her beauty was tempered now with worry and fatigue, the fine lines at the corners of her eyes and the dark smudges beneath them giving mute testimony to a life filled with unrelenting strain. Nor had her eyes lost their expressiveness—except that now they reflected disillusion and sadness instead of the love he remembered from that fateful night. Whatever burden she had carried for the past five years had clearly taken a tremendous toll on her, he concluded. She looked fragile. And achingly vulnerable. And very much alone. She seemed like a woman desperately in need of a shoulder to cry on or just a comforting hand to hold, he reflected, surprised—and disconcerted—by the unexpected surge of protectiveness that coursed through him.

Kate returned the doctor's stare, held by his compelling eyes. His gaze wasn't invasive or unfriendly—more like...unsettling. As if he knew something she didn't. Which was odd. They'd never met before, had they? she wondered, frowning slightly. Yet there *was* something familiar about him. But surely she would remember hair the color of sun-ripened wheat and eyes so intensely blue. Perhaps he just reminded her of someone from her past.

Eric realized that she didn't recognize him. Which wasn't surprising, in light of their traumatic "meeting"—if it could even be called that. And maybe it was just as well, considering his odd reaction on seeing her again. She drew him in a strangely powerful, inexplicable way; and that scared him. His divorce from Cindy four and half years before had taught him very clearly that marriage and medicine didn't mix. Since then he'd steered clear of serious relationships. It was a rule he'd never broken. And he wasn't going to start now—with *any* woman. So, with an effort, he put his professional smile in place and held out his hand.

"Mrs. Nolan? I'm Eric Carlson."

Kate found her fingers engulfed in a firm grip that somehow felt both capable and caring. "Hello, Doctor."

"And this must be Sarah." He squatted down beside the wary little girl, who was watching him solemnly, her eyes wide, as she clung to her mother. "Hello, Sarah. I'm Dr. Eric." When she didn't respond, he tried again. "You know, I have something in my office you might like to see when we're all finished. A big tank full of beautiful fish. What's your favorite color?"

"Pink."

"Well, I have a pink fish that has a bright blue tail. Would you like to see it later?"

Sarah studied him silently for a moment. "Are you going to give me a shot?"

Eric chuckled and glanced at Kate. "Nothing like cutting to the chase, is there?" Then he transferred his attention back to Sarah and shook his head. "Nope. No shots today. I promise. So how about letting me look in your ears and peek at your tonsils? And I'll let you listen to my heart if you let me listen to yours."

Sarah tipped her head and studied him for a moment before loosening her grip on Kate. "Okay."

"That's a girl." Eric reached over and picked her up, then settled her on the end of the table. From that point on, the exam proceeded smoothly. Eric even managed to elicit a giggle or two.

Kate watched in amazement, and her respect for Eric grew exponentially from minute to minute. He had a knack for putting children at ease, for making an exam fun, and she suspected that even on those occasions when he did have to give shots, he drew little protest from his patients. He had certainly befriended Sarah, Kate conceded. Her usually shy, reserved little girl was completely relaxed.

As he worked, Eric casually asked Kate a few astute, specific questions, never shifting his focus from Sarah. When he finished, he straightened and smiled down at his patient. "Now, that wasn't so bad, was it?"

Sarah shook her head. "It didn't hurt at all. I like you. He's nice, isn't he, Mommy?" she declared, looking over at Kate.

Kate cast an admiring glance at Eric. "Yes, honey, he sure is."

Eric felt his neck grow red at Kate's praise. Which was both odd and extremely unsettling. He never lost his cool with patients—or their mommies. To buy himself a moment to regain his composure, he lifted Sarah to the floor, then bent down to retrieve a wayward cotton ball.

Kate didn't know exactly what triggered the sudden flash of memory. Maybe it was Eric's motion of leaning so close to her, or the position of his body in conjunction with hers, or the way the overhead lighting suddenly drew out the burnished gold in his hair. But abruptly and with startling clarity she recalled another time, five years before, when this man had leaned over in exactly the same way as he'd worked on her critically injured husband in an icy wrecked car.

Her sudden gasp of recognition made Eric quickly straighten, and as their gazes met he realized that the odd link they shared was no longer a mystery to her.

Her face had gone a shade paler, and he noted the sudden trembling of her fingers as her hand went to her throat.

Eric forced his gaze from hers and smiled at Sarah. "Are you ready to see that pink fish now?"

Oblivious to the sudden undertones in the room, the little girl nodded eagerly and turned to Kate. "It's all right, isn't it, Mommy?"

Somehow Kate found her voice. "Yes."

Eric took Sarah's hand and looked over at Kate discerningly. "I'll be back in a moment. Will you be okay?"

She nodded mutely, still trying to process the bizarre coincidence of today's encounter. When her own pediatrician had retired a few weeks ago, she'd simply selected the most conveniently located replacement from the list he'd provided. Eric Carlson—the man who'd saved Jack's life.

Kate had always meant to find out the name of the doctor who had stopped that night to help, intending to write him a heartfelt letter of thanks. But as the months had gone by she'd been so overwhelmed by all the other demands in her life that she had never followed through. And especially in light of the outcome, which had left her in a deep depression for almost a year. It had been all she could do after that, simply to cope. There were days even now when that was all she did— cope. But that was no excuse. This man deserved better from her, and the guilt had nagged at her for years.

Eric slipped back into the room then and shut the door before taking a seat across from Kate.

"I left Sarah in my office with one of my assistants. She'll keep her occupied until we're finished."

"You were the doctor at the accident, weren't you?" Kate said without preamble.

Eric seemed momentarily taken aback by her abrupt words, then he slowly nodded. "Yes. I recognized you the minute I came in the door."

"I never thanked you. I meant to."

He shrugged. "No thanks were necessary. I'm a doctor. That's my job."

She shook her head vehemently. "No. You didn't even have to stop, especially considering the weather. I don't remember much about that night. I had a slight concussion, and everything has always been a blur. But they told me you saved Jack's life. I always intended to find out your name and let you know I appreciated what you did."

He made a dismissive gesture. "I just opened an airway. It was enough to give him a fighting chance until he got to the hospital." He glanced briefly at her left hand, noted the ring, then proceeded carefully. "Your husband seemed to be badly hurt, Mrs. Nolan."

She swallowed and gave a brief nod of confirmation. "Yes. Two vertebrae in his neck were crushed and he had severe head injuries. At first they weren't sure if he'd even make it through the night. He was in a coma and I just lived hour by hour. But he held on somehow. And with every day that passed I grew more hopeful, despite the fact that the doctors didn't offer much encouragement. They said even if he came out of the coma, he would be paralyzed. That he'd never be the way he was before. But I was sure they were wrong. I had great faith in those days." There was an unmistakable trace of bitterness in her voice, but it was replaced by bleakness when she continued. "We never had a chance to find out, though. He died seven months later without ever regaining consciousness.''

It was what Eric had feared. The desolate look in Kate's eyes, the slump of her shoulders, the catch in her voice, made his heart ache. "I'm sorry," he said helplessly, wishing he could take away her pain, offer some words of comfort. But he'd been through this before with other survivors, and he knew words did little to ease the burden of grief or the devastating sense of emptiness and loss that accompanied the death of a loved one. There was no way to make the absolute finality of that parting any less painful.

She blinked rapidly, and he saw the sheen of tears in her eyes. "Thank you. You'd think after four years I'd be able to handle it better than this, but...well, Jack and Sarah were my whole world. Sarah was only six weeks old when it happened, and we had so many plans, so much to look forward to...." Her voice trailed off and she sniffed, struggling for composure. At last she drew a shaky breath, and when she spoke her voice was choked and barely audible. "Everyone said I'd get over it. That life would go on and in time I'd feel back to normal. But you know, I don't think you ever get over it. You just get on with it."

Eric felt his throat tighten at the abject misery in Kate's eyes. "It takes a lot of courage just to do that," he told her gently, his own voice uneven.

She gave him a sad smile and shook her head. "It's kind of you to say that, Doctor. But it doesn't take courage to simply do what you have to do. Sarah needs me. Period. And I love her with all my heart. That's why these mysterious stomach pains have me so worried."

Eric couldn't change the tragedy that had brought Kate more than her share of heartache, but at least he could set her mind at ease about Sarah.

"Well, I don't think you need to worry, Mrs. Nolan. I can't find a thing wrong. She seems like a very healthy little girl."

"Then what's the problem?"

He toyed with his pencil for a moment, his face pensive. "Has there been any sort of trauma in her life recently?"

Kate nodded slowly as fresh tears sprang to her eyes. "Yes. My…my mother died very suddenly a month ago. She and Sarah were very close. We all were, actually. Sort of like The Three Musketeers."

Her voice quavered, and Eric's heart went out to her. She'd had so much loss. It didn't seem fair. He longed to ease her pain, but knew there was nothing he could do. Except listen.

Kate took a deep, shaky breath. "Anyway, Mom lived with us and watched Sarah for me during the school year while I was teaching. I had to find other day care for Sarah at the last minute, and she started a couple of weeks ago, right before I went back to school. It's been a big adjustment for her. For both of us, actually. You see, I always wanted to be home until she went to school. Jack and I had agreed on that. But of course things changed when he died. Having Mom watch her was the next best thing. Now… Well, I hate leaving her with strangers. Sarah is shy, and I'm afraid she may not be mixing well with the other children." Kate bit her lip, clearly distraught.

"You know, it sounds to me like her pains may be emotionally rather than physically triggered," Eric observed. "Coping with the loss of her grandmother was probably hard enough. Coupled with being thrust into a traditional day-care situation—well, it's a big adjustment. Are there any other options?"

Kate frowned and shook her head, her eyes deeply troubled. "This was the best I could do at the last minute. Most of the really good places are booked solid and have waiting lists a mile long." She dropped her head into her hands and drew a shuddering breath. "This isn't at all what I wanted for Sarah!"

Eric's throat tightened. For a brief moment he was overcome by a powerful urge to reach over and take her hand, to give her the reassurance of a caring touch that she seemed to need so desperately. He knew that she was stressed to the limit, torn between want and necessity. At this point he was actually more worried about *her* physical and emotional state than he was about Sarah's. Children had a way of adjusting. And Sarah had the security of Kate's love. But Kate was alone, with no one to share her burdens. Though his heart told him to reach out to her, in the end professional decorum prevailed and he refrained—with great effort.

"You're doing the best you can, Mrs. Nolan, under very difficult circumstances," he reassured her gently, his voice unusually husky. "Don't be too hard on yourself."

Kate looked into his eyes, and she felt strangely comforted by the kindness and compassion she saw there. She *was* trying to do her best, and it lifted her spirits ever-so-slightly to have someone recognize that.

"Thank you. But it's obviously not good enough. I want what's best for Sarah, Doctor. There has to be a better solution than this." She sighed and wearily ran her fingers through her shoulder-length hair. "I guess I'll just have to keep looking."

Eric stared at her bowed head, his face growing thoughtful as an idea suddenly took shape his mind. If he could pull it off, several problems would be solved, he realized. Sarah would have a more personal day-care situation. Kate's guilt would be eased. And Eric's mind would be relieved of a constant worry. It was a long shot, of course. And he didn't want to raise any expectations until he had a commitment. But it just might work.

"I'm sure you'll find the answer, Mrs. Nolan. And in the meantime, remember that children are more resilient than we think. You're clearly a caring, conscientious parent, and children know intuitively when they're loved. That makes a huge difference."

Kate looked at Eric, essentially a stranger to her despite their brief, traumatic encounter five years before. Yet he seemed to know exactly the right thing to say to relieve her mind. Maybe it was a knack he had with all worried mothers. But the caring in his eyes seemed genuine—and somehow personal. Which was silly, of course. She was just another case to him. But she appreciated his kindness nonetheless.

"You have a great bedside manner, Doctor. Even if I'm not the patient," she told him with a tremulous smile. "I feel much better."

He returned the smile, and she liked the way his eyes crinkled at the corners. "I'm glad. And let me know if Sarah is still having problems in a week or so. But I think she'll adjust, given time."

"I just wish there was another option," Kate said with a sigh.

Eric didn't comment as he stood and ushered her to the door. But he had a plan. And if everything went as he hoped, Kate's wish just might come true.

Anna Carlson's hand froze, the glass of orange juice halfway to her mouth, as she stared at her son over the plate of scrambled eggs.

"You want me to do what?"

Eric had known it wasn't going to be an easy sell. Ever since his father had died six months before, his mother had shut herself off from the world, struggling not only with grief over the passing of her lifelong companion but also with a sense of uselessness. A nurturer by disposition, she had found her meaning in life by caring for the men she loved—Eric when he was younger, and in recent years her husband, as failing health made him increasingly dependent. In fact, their already strong mutual devotion had seemed to intensify as Walter's physical condition weakened.

While some women would resent the demands of living with an ill spouse, Anna had never complained. As she'd told her son on more than one occasion, "Walter took care of us for a lot of years, Eric. He worked three jobs at once when you were a baby just to make ends meet. Nothing was too much trouble if it made life easier for the people he loved. How can I do any less now, when he needs me?"

Now, with his father gone and the demands of his practice keeping him too busy to give his mother as much time as he'd like, she was adrift. The inspired idea he'd had in the office a couple of days before had seemed like the perfect solution for everyone. His mother needed someone to take care of. Sarah needed someone to do just that. Kate needed the peace of mind that a good caregiver would provide. And he wanted to help his mother find new purpose in life. It was an ideal arrangement.

But from the way she was staring at him, one would think he'd suggested she take up skydiving.

"I'd like you to consider watching one of my patients five days a week during school hours while her mother teaches," he repeated evenly.

His mother set her glass down and continued to stare at him. "Why on earth would I what to do that?"

Eric mulled over his response while the server poured him a fresh cup of coffee and decided on the direct approach.

"She needs help, Mom."

Anna frowned at him. "Who? The mother or the little girl?"

"Both."

Even if she wasn't exactly receptive, he'd at least aroused her curiosity, Eric thought. His mother hadn't looked this interested in anything since before his father had died. Their after-church Sunday-morning breakfasts had become a ritual during the last six months. It was a time he reserved exclusively for her, but usually she was subdued and barely picked at her food. Today he'd managed to snap her out of her apathy, if only for a few moments.

In fact, as she studied him now, he began to grow slightly uncomfortable. He knew that look. It was one he remembered well from his growing-up years, when she was trying to figure out what was going on in his mind, what his motivation was. Her next question confirmed it.

"Eric, in all the years you've been a doctor, I've never seen you take such a personal interest in a patient. Is there something you're not telling me about this situation?"

He had to give her credit. She was as sharp and insightful as ever. He'd never told her about the accident, but he did so now, as briefly as possible and characteristically downplaying his role. She listened with interest, and when he'd finished she looked at him shrewdly.

"And your paths just suddenly crossed again two days ago?"

"Yes."

She pondered that for a moment. "It seems odd, doesn't it?"

"Very."

"Even so, there's really no reason for you to get involved in this woman's life, is there? You must meet a lot of parents who are facing similar dilemmas."

He couldn't argue with that. Broken families, single-parent households, stepchildren—and the many problems they entailed—he'd seen it all. And he'd never before been tempted to intervene personally. At least not to this extent. His mother was right. There wasn't any reason to get involved in Kate Nolan's life. Except maybe one: he wanted to. And at the moment he wasn't inclined to analyze his motivation.

"Let's just say that I think it would be the Christian thing to do," he replied noncommittally. "You have the time. She has the need. It's the right combination

of circumstances at the right time. There's nothing
more to it than that.''

His mother looked skeptical, but she didn't belabor
the point. Instead she glanced down at her plate and
poked at her scrambled eggs, a thoughtful frown on her
face. Eric waited quietly, praying that she'd at least
give this a chance. It would be as good for her as it
would be for Kate and Sarah.

When at last she met his gaze, her own was still
uncertain. ''I don't know, Eric. It's a big responsibility.
And they're strangers to me. What if we don't even
like each other?''

''You'll like them, Mom. I guarantee it. And they'll
love you. Sarah misses her grandmother, and I can't
think of a better surrogate. You were made for that
role.''

And this was the only chance she would have to play
it. The unspoken words hung in the air between them.
Eric's marriage had produced no children, much to his
regret. And there wouldn't be another. He had made
his peace with that. Anna never had. She thought he
needed a wife, and she occasionally dropped broad
hints to that effect when the opportunity presented itself. As she did now.

''I haven't given up on having a real grandchild, you
know,'' she said pointedly.

''It's time you did.''

''You're only thirty-eight, Eric. It's not too late to
have a family.''

''Mom.'' There was a warning note in his voice,
which Anna ignored.

''Of course, you'd need a wife first.''

''I have a wife.''

"You've been divorced for almost five years, Eric."

"You know how I feel about that."

Anna sighed and glanced at the wedding band on his left hand. "Yes, I guess I do."

Eric knew that most people considered divorce a perfectly acceptable solution for a troubled union, that they found his attitude archaic. As did even his mother, who didn't take divorce lightly. But he believed in the sanctity of marriage; believed that the vows so solemnly taken were for life. He and Cindy might be divorced on paper, but in the eyes of God he believed they were still man and wife. Even Cindy's remarriage three years before hadn't convinced him otherwise. He wasn't going to judge her. He left that to the Lord. But it wasn't the right thing for him. Besides, his dedication to his career had ruined one marriage. He wasn't about to inflict that burden on another woman. In the meantime, they'd wandered far from the subject at hand.

"None of this has any bearing on our discussion, Mom," he pointed out. "If you're worried about whether you'll all get along, then how about this—I'll call Kate Nolan, and if she's interested I'll arrange for her to stop by and visit you. That way, the two of you can size each other up and you can meet Sarah. How does that sound?"

Anna nodded slowly. "I suppose I could consider it. But I'm not making any promises, Eric."

"I don't expect you to."

"I do feel sorry for her, though. So many burdens on someone so young. How old did you say Sarah was when the accident happened?"

"Six weeks."

His mother shook her head. "I can't even imagine.

It's enough of a challenge for two people to raise a child. But for a single working mother... And then to lose her own mother so recently. She really does sound like she needs help, Eric.''

"She does. She's been living under tremendous strain for years. I'd say she's approaching the danger level on the stress scale.''

"Well, I suppose I could meet her, at least. Maybe help her out until she finds someone to take over permanently.''

Eric felt the tension in his shoulders ease. "I know she'd appreciate it, Mom.''

"This is all contingent on whether we get along, though,'' his mother cautioned.

"You'll get along fine.''

"How can you be so sure?''

"Because I know you.''

"But you don't know Kate Nolan. You just met her.''

"Let's just call it intuition.''

Eric was relieved that his mother seemed to accept that response. Even it if wasn't quite true. Because, odd as it seemed, he felt as if he *did* know Kate Nolan. But he couldn't very well tell his mother that. She would jump to all sorts of conclusions—all of them wrong, of course.

Weren't they?

Chapter Two

Kate pulled to a stop in front of the small, tidy brick bungalow and took a slow, steadying breath. She still wasn't sure how all this had come about.

Two days ago, when Eric Carlson had called to check on Sarah, Kate had been impressed by his conscientiousness. No doctor she'd seen before had ever personally followed up with a phone call after an office visit. She'd hardly recovered from that pleasant surprise when he'd gone on to say that he might have a solution to her day-care problem. To put it mildly, she'd been overwhelmed.

Even now, it was difficult to believe that he had gone to so much trouble, especially for a new patient. And by enlisting the aid of his own mother, no less! Of course, the way he'd carefully explained it to Kate, she'd be doing *him* a favor if this all worked out. Apparently his mother had been quite despondent since the death of Eric's father, and he was convinced that if she had someone to nurture—namely Sarah—she'd regain some sense of purpose in life.

He might be right, Kate mused. Feeling needed did wonders to help one through the day. But as far as she was concerned, *she* was the one who had the most to gain from this arrangement. Of course, Kate had to feel comfortable with Eric's mother. That was imperative. But almost anything would be an improvement over her current arrangement. Besides, she was sure the woman's character would be impeccable. If she had raised a man as fine as Eric seemed to be, how could she be anything less than stellar?

The stifling heat and humidity of the St. Louis summer slammed against Kate with a force that almost took her breath away as she stepped out of the car. It was a bit late in the season for such sauna-like conditions, but then again, in St. Louis you never knew. It was too bad the weather had decided to act up today, though. The classrooms at the school where she taught weren't air-conditioned, and she felt totally wilted and drained. On top of everything else, Sarah was cranky after another obviously unpleasant day at the day-care center—not the best time to make a good first impression, Kate thought ruefully. But it was too late to change the appointment now.

"Come on, honey, it will be cool in the house," she told Sarah encouragingly as she unbuckled her daughter's seat belt, then reached for her hand.

"I want to go home," Sarah whimpered, holding back.

"I know, honey. So do I. But I promised Dr. Eric we'd stop and visit his mommy. She's lonesome here all by herself. And we wouldn't want to break our promise to Dr. Eric, would we?''

Sarah wasn't in the mood for logic—or guilt trips.

"I don't want to," she declared stubbornly.

Kate's head began to pound. "We won't stay long. But I promised Dr. Eric. We have to go in," she told Sarah, struggling to keep her voice calm as she gently but firmly pulled her protesting daughter from the car.

"I don't want to!" Sarah wailed, resisting Kate's efforts.

"Sarah! Stop whining!" she ordered sharply, her patience evaporating. "We're going to go in. Now. And we'll be done a lot faster if you cooperate."

Sarah was still whimpering miserably as they made their way up the brick walkway. Despite her terse tone of moments before, Kate could empathize. She was so wrung out from the heat and the stress of the last few weeks that she felt like doing exactly the same thing. Instead, she forced herself to pay attention to her surroundings. She noted the large trees and fenced backyard—a perfect place for a child, she reflected appreciatively. Lots of shade and plenty of room to run and play. And Eric's mother lived just ten minutes away from her apartment. If only things would work out! She needed a few breaks—desperately. So did Sarah.

As a result, for the first time in a very long while, Kate made a request of the Lord. For Sarah's sake. She'd stopped praying for herself long ago, when He'd ignored her entreaties and abandoned her. But maybe He'd listen on behalf of a child. *Let this work out,* she pleaded silently. *I want what's best for Sarah, and I don't know where else to turn.*

As Kate pressed the doorbell, she glanced down at

her daughter. Sarah still looked hot and unhappy and ill-tempered. Kate just hoped that once inside, where it was cool, she'd settle down and give Eric's mother a glimpse of the charming little girl she usually was.

The door was pulled open almost immediately, leaving Kate to wonder if the older woman had been hovering on the inside of the door as anxiously as she was standing on the outside. For a moment they looked at each other, each rapidly taking inventory. Eric looked nothing like his mother, Kate noted immediately. This woman's hair was mostly gray, though traces of faded auburn revealed its original color—a contrast to Eric's gold blond. While Eric was tall—at least six feet—his mother was of moderate height. Five-five at the most, in heels, Kate estimated. And Eric had a trim, athletic build, while his mother was softly rounded. But she had a nice face, Kate decided. And her eyes were kind.

"You must be Kate," Anna said at last, her initial polite smile softening into true warmth.

"Yes. And this is Sarah."

Anna looked down at the little girl who eyed her warily.

"My! You're much more grown-up than I expected. I'm so glad you and your mommy decided to visit me today. It's always nice to make new friends, isn't it? Why don't you both come in before you melt and we'll have something cold to drink."

She moved aside, and Kate stepped into the welcome coolness.

"Oh, it feels wonderful in here!" she exclaimed with a sigh.

"It sure is a hot one out there today," Anna commiserated as she led the way into the living room.

"Eric tells me you teach. I certainly hope the school is air-conditioned."

Kate made a wry face. "No such luck. But I'll survive. This heat can't last forever."

"Well, let me get you both something to perk you up." She looked at Sarah, who sat quietly close beside Kate on the couch. "Now, I'll just bet you're the kind of girl who likes ice cream. Am I right?" Sarah nodded. "That's what I thought. Let me see—chocolate chip, that would be my guess."

Sarah's eyes grew wide. "That's my favorite."

"Mine, too. How about a nice big bowl to help you cool off? That is, if it's okay with your mother." She glanced at Kate, who smiled and nodded. "Good. I'll just run out to the kitchen and get it ready. Would you like to come, too? I have a parakeet you might like to meet."

Sarah looked at her curiously. "What's a para— parakeet?"

"Why, it's the most beautiful bird! Sometimes he even talks. His name is George. Would you like to see him?" Sarah nodded, and when Anna held out her hand the little girl took it shyly. The older woman looked over at Kate. "I'll get Sarah settled in the kitchen with her ice cream, and then we can have a little chat. Would you like some iced tea?"

"I'd love some," Kate replied gratefully. "Thank you."

Kate watched them leave. It must run in the family, this ability to make friends so easily with children, she marveled. Eric certainly had the gift. And now she knew where he got it. She listened to the animated chatter coming from the kitchen, and took a moment to look around the living room. It was a cozy space, neat as a pin but not too fussy. The furniture was comfortable and overstuffed—made for sitting in, not just looking at. Fresh flowers stood in a vase on the coffee table, and family photos were artfully arranged on the mantel.

Kate's gaze lingered on the pictures, and she rose and moved closer to examine them. She started at one end, with a black-and-white wedding photo—probably Anna and her husband, Kate speculated. Then came a picture of the same couple cutting a twenty-fifth-anniversary cake. Eric's father looked like a nice man, Kate reflected. And it was clear now where Eric got his looks. His father was tall, dignified, blond and blue-eyed—in other words, an older version of Eric.

But it wasn't photos of Anna and her husband that dominated the mantel. It was pictures of their son. Eric as a baby. Eric in a cub-scout uniform. Eric in a cap and gown, flanked by his proud parents. Eric with his parents again, in a shot of more recent vintage, taken on the deck of a cruise ship. And on the wall next to the mantel, a framed newspaper clipping about Eric having been named Man of the Year by a local charitable organization. Clearly, he was his parents' pride and joy.

But there was something missing from this gallery, Kate suddenly realized. Eric wore a wedding band. She remembered noticing it in the office, when he'd been playing with his pen. But there was nothing here to indicate that he had a wife, or a family. Or that he ever had. Curious.

Just then Anna returned, and Kate turned guiltily

from the mantel, her face flushed. "I hope you don't mind. I was admiring your pictures."

"Not at all," Anna assured her as she deposited a tray holding iced tea and a plate of cookies on the coffee table. "That's what they're there for. Now, I think we can relax and have a chat. Sarah is trying to get George to talk, and I also left her with some crayons and paper and asked her to draw me some pictures of him. That should keep her busy for a few minutes, anyway."

"You and your son both have a way with children," Kate said as a compliment to her as she returned to her seat.

"Well, it's not hard with a lovely little girl like that."

Kate grinned. "She wasn't so lovely a few minutes ago. I practically had to drag her in here. I figured you'd take one look and say, 'No way.' I think she had a rough day at day care." Her smile quickly faded.

"I guess that's what we're here to talk about," Anna replied. "Eric tells me that your mother used to watch her, until she passed away a month ago. I'm so very sorry about that, my dear. The loss of a mother is one of life's greatest trials."

The sincere sympathy in the older woman's voice brought a lump to Kate's throat, and she struggled to contain her tears. With all the turmoil since her mother's death—the disruption in the placid routine of their days, her worry about how Sarah was handling the death, and the necessity of making last-minute arrangements for her daughter's care—she'd had little time to grieve. But the ache of loss was heavy in her heart.

"Thank you. Mom and I were always close, but during these last few years since she came to live with us we forged an even stronger bond. My dad died about eight years ago, and Mom sold the farm in Ohio where we grew up and moved to an apartment in Cincinnati. She came to help out while Jack—my husband—was in the hospital, and when he died, she just stayed on. It was the best possible arrangement for all of us under the circumstances."

"You must miss her very much."

Kate nodded. The loneliness of her life had been thrown into stark relief by the death of her mother. Even her weekly phone calls to her sister didn't ease her sense of isolation.

"It was hard enough when Jack died. But Mom was there for me to lean on. Now... Well, it's just me. And Sarah, of course. She's such a joy to me. A lifeline, really. Even more precious because we never thought she'd happen. My husband and I tried for five years before we had her. We'd almost given up when we discovered I was pregnant. And we both agreed that I'd stay home at least until she went to school. We were firm believers that mothering is a full-time job."

Anna nodded approvingly. "I often think young mothers today make a mistake when they try to have it all. Not that you can't, of course. I just don't think you can have it all at the same time. 'To everything there is a season.' And children need full-time mothers, unless there are extraordinary circumstances."

"I agree completely. But as it turned out, I was faced with those extraordinary circumstances. I guess Eric told you what happened."

"He filled me in on the basics. I understand you lost your husband shortly after Sarah was born."

Kate nodded. "It was a nightmare. The accident happened on our first night out together since Sarah was born. We'd had an early dinner to celebrate our sixth anniversary."

"Oh, my dear! I had no idea. How awful!" Anna's face registered shock and sympathy.

"Unfortunately, the worst was still to come," Kate continued, her voice flat and lifeless. "Jack lived for seven months, but he never regained consciousness. By the time he died our finances were pretty much depleted. Long-term care is very expensive, and insurance doesn't cover everything. So I went back to teaching, sold our house and moved into an apartment. We've coped till now, but when Mom died, everything just fell apart again." Her voice caught on the last word, and she paused to take a deep breath, struggling to keep her tears at bay. Her voice was shaky when she continued. "I just can't bear to see Sarah so unhappy. That's why I'm desperate to find a more personal, one-on-one day-care situation. Someone who can give her the love and affection and attention that I would give her if I could be there. I guess your son thought you might be willing to pinch-hit, at least until I can find something more permanent. I'm hoping the same thing," she admitted frankly.

Anna carefully set her iced-tea glass on a coaster and looked at Kate, her face concerned. "I'd like to help you, my dear. But you do understand that I'm not experienced in day care, don't you?"

Kate smiled. "You're a mother. And you raised a fine son, from what I can see. You seem kind and caring. And Sarah seems to have taken to you. Those are good enough credentials for me.'' Kate had decided after five minutes in her presence that Anna was the answer to her prayer.

"Well, as Eric told me, this might be my one and only chance to play grandmother,'' the older woman reflected. ''And I would enjoy that.''

Kate looked at her curiously. ''What do you mean?''

"Eric's divorced. Has been for almost five years. He and Cindy never had any children. Pity, too, when he loves children so much.''

"But he might remarry.''

Anna shook her head sadly. ''Not Eric. So perhaps I'd best take my opportunity.''

Kate was curious about Anna's enigmatic comment regarding Eric, but her attention was focused on the woman's second statement. She looked at her hopefully, her own heart banging painfully in her chest. ''Does that mean you'll watch Sarah?''

Anna nodded. ''At least for a while. Just tell me what kind of schedule you're thinking about.''

Within ten minutes the details were settled, and Kate looked across at Anna. ''I can't ever thank you enough for this, Mrs. Carlson. I feel like such a great burden has been lifted from my mind.''

"First of all, it's Anna. And I'm glad I can help you with this. It seems like you've had far too many trials for someone so young.''

"I don't feel very young these days,'' Kate admitted wearily. ''I may only be thirty-six, but sometimes I feel ancient.''

Suddenly Sarah burst into the room to proudly show off her drawings of George. As Anna exclaimed over them, Kate settled back with her iced tea. Once upon a time, Eric had saved her husband's life. In many ways, Kate felt he had just now saved hers. And in her heart she knew that she owed him a debt of gratitude she could never even begin to repay.

"So what happened?"

"I'm fine, thanks. How are you?" Anna's amused voice came over the wire.

"Sorry," Eric apologized sheepishly. "It's just that I've had your meeting with Mrs. Nolan on my mind all afternoon, and this is the first chance I've had to call."

"It's seven-thirty. It must have been a busy day."

"It was. I had an emergency at the hospital that delayed me."

He heard her exasperated sigh. "You work too hard, Eric. Especially since the divorce. I admire your dedication, but you need to have a life, too."

They'd been over this before—countless times. After Cindy had left and he'd decided that marriage and medicine didn't mix, he'd immersed himself in his work to the exclusion of just about everything else. He knew it wasn't healthy. He knew he needed to back off from some of his commitments, resign from a couple of the boards he was on, give some serious thought to his partner's suggestion that they bring another doctor into their practice. And he'd get around to all those things one of these days. In the meantime, he was more worried about the stress level of one beautiful-but-sad mother and her little girl.

"You're changing the subject, Mom."

"Well, I worry about you."

"Worry about Mrs. Nolan and Sarah instead. They need it more than I do."

She sighed again. "Yes, I think you're right. Oh, Eric, the minute I opened the door and looked at them, my heart just about broke. Sarah is such a precious, sensitive child. I can see where she'd feel lost in one of those big day-care centers. And Kate... Oh, dear, that poor woman. What a tragic story! And to have that accident happen on her wedding anniversary—I can't even imagine the horror. Anyway, she looked so lost and alone, standing there on the porch. And so tired and anxious. I just wanted to hug her."

Eric could relate to that. He'd felt exactly the same way. "So you agreed to watch Sarah?"

"How could I refuse? As you said, it just seemed like the Christian thing to do. Besides, I liked them both. It won't be a hardship."

"When do you start?"

"Tomorrow."

Eric's eyebrows rose in surprise. "Pretty fast action."

"Why wait? I don't have anything planned, and Kate can't get her daughter out of that place fast enough. Of course, I had to run to the store and pick up a few things. Peanut butter and jelly, ingredients for my sugar cookies, some coloring books and Play-Doh. You know, that kind of thing. I'm not used to entertaining a child."

There was a new energy in his mother's voice, an enthusiasm that Eric hadn't heard in months. Apparently his instinct that this arrangement would be good for everyone had been right on target, he thought with satisfaction.

"Do you need me to do anything?"

"No. I have it all under control, thanks."

"Well, I'll see you Sunday, then. And good luck."

"Thanks. I think things will work out just fine."

So did Eric. He was happy for his mother and Kate and Sarah—and strangely enough, for himself, as well. He wasn't quite sure why. Perhaps because now he could stop worrying so much about his mother. He could use some peace of mind on that score.

But there were other things about this arrangement that *weren't* conducive to peace of mind, he suddenly realized. Such as the link it provided with Kate Nolan. For reasons he preferred to leave unexplored, he didn't think that would necessarily lead to mental serenity.

"You know, one of these days I'm going to stop inviting you, since you never come, but Mary said I should try one more time. So...barbecue, Labor Day, five o'clock. What's your excuse this time?"

Eric slid the chart back into the folder and grinned at his partner. Frank Shapiro seemed the complete opposite of his colleague. Six inches shorter, with close-cropped, thinning brown hair and a wiry build, Frank exuded high energy in contrast to Eric's calm demeanor. While Frank was an outgoing extrovert, Eric stayed more to himself. But as they'd discovered during their residency together, in every other way—philosophical, ethical, political, religious—they were a good match. Their partnership had flourished, and Eric had only one complaint. Since his divorce, Frank had been unrelenting in his attempts to spice up Eric's practically nonexistent social life. Eric had always deflected his efforts, but he suddenly decided to throw his friend a curve.

"No excuse. I'll be there."

Frank stared at him. "What?"

"I said I'll come."

Frank tilted his head and looked at Eric suspiciously. "Are you serious?"

"Uh-huh."

"Well...gosh, that's great! Wait till I tell Mary our persistence finally paid off."

"Can I bring anything?"

"No, thanks. Except a date, that is." Frank grinned.

Eric grinned back. His friend was joking, of course. Frank knew he never dated. But suddenly Eric thought of Kate Nolan, and his expression grew thoughtful. He suspected she had even less of a social life than he did; that she rarely, if ever, allowed herself a night out, and that there was very little laughter and lightheartedness in her world. Not much of a life for a young, vital woman. Maybe he ought to ask her.

Eric frowned. Now where had that idea come from? What about his rule of keeping personal involvements at arm's length? Exceptions weren't a good idea, he told himself firmly. And yet, for some reason, ever since Kate had walked into his office he'd felt a sense of...*responsibility*—that was the word—for her. He couldn't explain it. Didn't even try. It was just there. And it nudged him to invite her. Just as a friend, of course. It would be an act of charity. Nothing more.

He laid the folder on the counter and purposely kept his tone casual. "I just might do that."

The look of surprise on Frank's face was almost

comical. He stared at his partner for several seconds before he found his voice.

"Well...that's great!" He clearly wanted to ask more, but for once he seemed momentarily at a loss for words. And Eric didn't give him a chance to recover.

"On to the next patient," he declared, picking up a chart. As he walked away he could sense Frank staring after him, the dumbfounded look still on his face. And Eric couldn't help grinning. Everyone figured he was so predictable. Well, maybe it was time he started surprising a few people.

Then again, maybe it wasn't, Eric ruminated glumly as he stared at the phone in his office on Friday evening. The party was only three days away, and he still hadn't summoned up the courage to call Kate Nolan. What on earth had prompted him to make that impetuous remark to Frank? He should have been content with Frank's initial surprise when he'd accepted the invitation. There had been no need for overkill, he chastised himself.

And now he was stuck. Frank expected him to show up with a date in tow, and he'd never hear the end of it if he didn't. His partner would badger him about the "mystery" woman he'd "almost" brought. Even worse, thinking he was now willing to date, Frank would renew his efforts to set his friend up, much as he had—relentlessly—for a year or two after the divorce. Eric closed his eyes and groaned. He loved Frank. Like a brother. But not when he played matchmaker. No, he had to show up with someone. And Kate Nolan was the only option.

Besides, there were altruistic reasons for this invitation, he rationalized. Kate seemed to lead far too solitary a life. As far as he could see, she only had Sarah. The little girl was a charmer, he acknowledged, and she seemed to adequately fulfill her mother's nurturing needs. But what about Kate's other needs? Despite the tragedy that had taken the man she loved, she still needed adult companionship. And adult conversation. And someone who cared when she had a cold or a taxing day, who worried when she worked too hard or didn't eat right. He was certain those needs weren't being met. Inviting her to go with him to Frank's party wasn't a solution—but it might be a step toward a more normal, balanced life for her.

Feeling more confident, he picked up the phone and dialed her number, tapping his pen restlessly against the desk as he waited. When she answered, three rings later and out of breath, his hand stilled.

"Mrs. Nolan? It's Eric Carlson." That was odd. He sounded as breathless as she did.

There was a momentary pause, and he could sense her surprise, could imagine the look of astonishment on her face. His assessment of her reaction was confirmed by her tone of voice when she spoke.

"Hello, Doctor." He heard her draw a deep breath. "I was just opening the door when the phone rang. I had to run to answer it." *And why are you calling me?* The question, though unasked, hung in the air.

"I wanted to thank you for the note you sent me." She'd written him a warm, heartfelt letter after Anna had agreed to watch Sarah, and it suddenly seemed like a good way to open the conversation.

"Oh. You're welcome. I was very grateful for everything you did."

"I'm just glad it worked out. Mom seems much more like her old self, even though it's only been a week."

"Well, speaking for Sarah, this seems like a match made in heaven. She and your mom hit it off right from the beginning. Her morning tune has changed from 'Do I have to go?' to 'Hurry up, Mom. We'll be late for Aunt Anna's.' In fact, I'm not sure how she'll manage away from your mom for three whole days over the Labor Day holiday."

That gave him the opening he needed. "Maybe she doesn't have to."

He could hear the frown in Kate's voice. "What do you mean?"

Eric took a deep breath and willed his racing pulse to slow down. You'd think he'd never asked a woman out before, he thought with chagrin. And this wasn't even a real date, anyway.

"Well, I know this is a bit last-minute, but I was wondering if you were free Monday. My partner is having a barbecue, and I thought it might be a nice change of pace for you, after the stress of the last few weeks. And I could use a break myself."

Her stunned silence conveyed her reaction more eloquently than words. Well, what did he expect? he asked himself wryly. After all, they barely knew each other. In her position he'd probably react the same way. And he'd likely decline. So before she could do so, he spoke again, playing his trump card.

"I'm sure you're surprised by the invitation, but to be honest, you'd do me a real favor if you'd accept.

Frank is a great guy, but he's always trying to fix me up and I'd like to avoid that. I'm just not interested in dating, and I can't seem to convince him of that. I usually turn down his invitations, but I figured if I came to one of his parties with a date, he might decide I could take care of my own social life after all and would lay off.''

Kate stared at the phone, a frown marring her brow, her refusal dying on her lips. She wasn't in the dating mode and never would be again. What was the point, when she'd already had the best? That kind of love only came around once in a lifetime. Though Jack might be gone in body, she'd never let him go in her heart. He was her husband. He was Sarah's father. And no one could take his place. Ever. Period. She'd never even looked at another man since his death, let alone dated one. And she saw no reason to start now.

But then Eric had added that caveat: that she'd be doing him a favor by saving him from the well-meaning-but-unwanted matchmaking efforts of his friend. Then he'd gone on to say that he wasn't interested in dating, either. His mother had implied the same thing at their first meeting, Kate recalled. And she owed him—big time, after what he'd done to help her resolve her day-care dilemma. So what would be the harm in accepting his invitation? Nothing that she could articulate. Yet somehow it didn't feel quite right. The notion of spending an evening in Eric's company made her...uneasy.

As the silence lengthened, Kate realized she had to say something. And honesty seemed the best approach. ''I don't know, Doctor,'' she replied frankly, toying with the phone cord as she spoke. ''I try to spend all my free time with Sarah. And I'd have to find someone to watch her.''

''That's where Mom comes in. She'd be happy to look after Sarah.''

''You mean…you already asked your mother?'' She was clearly taken aback.

''Uh-huh.'' He'd checked with her before he'd called Kate, wanting to remove any potential stumbling blocks in advance.

''Oh. Well, wasn't she…surprised?''

''Actually, no.'' Which had surprised *him*. He'd expected to be plied with questions when he'd made the request. Instead, his mother had simply said, ''No problem.'' And frankly, that had made him a little nervous. It wasn't like her. But instead of pressing his luck, he'd simply said thanks and ended the conversation as soon as possible, before she slipped back into character and launched into the third degree.

''Oh.'' Kate was starting to sound like George, who had a tendency to repeat the same words over and over again, she realized. ''Well, I do have school the next day.''

''We can make it an early night.''

It was getting harder and harder to think of excuses. Eric was being absolutely cooperative and understanding. How could she say no? With a sigh, Kate capitulated. ''All right, Doctor. If it will help you out.''

He closed his eyes and let out a long, slow breath. When he spoke again, she heard the teasing tone in his voice.

''There's just one thing.''

''What?''

''I don't think this is going to work too well if you

call me 'Doctor.' Frank might smell a rat, don't you think?''

Kate found herself smiling. "You could be right."

"So...how about if we switch to Eric and Kate?"

"I just hope I don't forget. I'm used to thinking of you as 'Doctor.'''

"I may have the same problem. Be sure to elbow me if I call you Mrs. Nolan."

But he wouldn't. Because oddly enough, since the moment she'd walked into his office she'd been "Kate" to him. In fact, he'd had to remind himself to call her "Mrs. Nolan." So this switch would be no problem at all.

"All right, Doct— Eric," she corrected herself.

They settled on a time, and as Eric replaced the receiver and leaned back in his chair, he experienced an odd combination of emotions. Relief. Satisfaction. Anticipation. Uncertainty. And last, but certainly not least, guilt.

He frowned over that last one. Why did he suddenly have this niggling sensation of guilt? He wasn't doing anything wrong. Professional ethics kept doctors from dating patients, but he knew of no such sanction against *mommies* of patients. And he hadn't exerted too much pressure on Kate. If she'd resisted too much, he would have backed off. The last thing she needed in her life was more stress. Finally, while it was true that he refrained from dating because he believed that in the eyes of the Lord he was still married, this wasn't a real date.

So why did he feel guilty? After all, he was doing this for her. Out of compassion. As a friend. He felt sorry for her. It was as simple as that.

Or was it? he asked himself. Because if his motives were so noble and unselfish, if he was only thinking of *her,* why was *he* looking forward to the barbecue so much?

Chapter Three

Kate glanced in the mirror behind her bedroom door and absently adjusted the strap on her sundress. She'd been so taken aback by Dr. Carlson's—Eric's, she reminded herself—invitation that she hadn't thought to ask about attire. Was she too dressed up? What did people wear to a barbecue these days? It had been years since she'd been to one. To any purely social function, in fact. It actually felt odd to be dressing up for a night out. Odd—and a little uncomfortable.

Kate frowned. Even though Eric had made it clear that this wasn't a date, it had all the trappings of one. And that made her conscience twinge, as if she were somehow cheating on Jack. Which was ridiculous, of course. She loved Jack absolutely, with a devotion that was undimmed by the years. She was simply doing a favor for someone who had gone out of his way to be kind to her. There was no reason to feel guilty, she admonished herself sternly.

Resolutely she picked up her purse and stepped into

the hall. Sarah glanced up from her perch on the couch and smiled as Kate approached.

"You look pretty, Mommy."

"Thanks, honey."

"I wish I could go to the party, too."

Kate's heart contracted and she sat down beside Sarah. She already felt incredibly guilty about leaving her daughter with a sitter—even if it *was* Anna—on a weekend, and Sarah's innocent comment was enough to send a pang through her heart. For just a moment she was tempted to back out on Eric. But she owed him this, she reminded herself. Just as she owed Sarah as much time as possible on her days off to make up for all the hours during the week when they had to be apart. It was a perennial dilemma, this conflict between her daughter's needs and other obligations. But she *had* promised Eric. And Sarah would be fine for one night with Anna, she assured herself.

"I wish you could, too, honey. But it's a grown-up party. And when Dr. Eric asked me to go with him I thought I should, since he was so nice to us. If it wasn't for Dr. Eric, we would never have met Aunt Anna," Kate reminded her, using the affectionate title for the older woman that she and Anna had decided upon.

"I like Aunt Anna," Sarah declared. "She said we would make cookies tonight and watch *Mary Poppins*. Have you seen that movie, Mommy?"

"Uh-huh. You'll like it. And I might even be back before it's over."

The doorbell rang, and Kate reached over to give Sarah a quick hug. "That's Dr. Eric now. Run and get your sweater and then we'll take you over to Aunt Anna's."

As Sarah scampered toward her bedroom, Kate rose and walked slowly to the door. She still felt ill at ease, but she tried to suppress her nervousness. After all, Eric seemed like a nice man. He wasn't looking for anything more than companionship. And she *had* been a pretty good conversationalist at one time, even if her skills were a bit rusty. Maybe she'd even have fun, she told herself encouragingly. But she knew that possibility was remote. Fun didn't play much of a role in her life these days. She reached for the knob and sighed. Wouldn't it be nice, though, if—

The sight of Eric's broad shoulders filling her doorway cut off her thought in mid-sentence and her polite smile of welcome froze on her face. He looked different today, she thought inanely, her lips parting slightly in surprise as she stared at him. More...human. And he exuded a virility that had been camouflaged beneath his clinical demeanor, white coat and stethoscope during their last encounter in his office. At work he looked professional and slightly remote, and his role was clear. In his present attire—khaki trousers and a cobalt-blue golf shirt that hugged his muscular chest and matched the color of his eyes—he seemed to be playing a much less precisely defined role. It was an unsettling and intimidating change. Yet his eyes—warm and genuine and straightforward, even while reflecting some other emotion she couldn't quite put her finger on—helped to calm her jitters.

Eric watched the play of emotions on Kate's face as he struggled to control his own expression. Her smile of welcome had faded to a look of surprise, and her slightly parted lips, along with the pulse that began to beat in the delicate hollow of her throat, clearly communicated her nervousness. She looked vulnerable and scared...and very, very appealing, he thought, as his heart stopped, then raced on. By anyone's definition, her simple sundress was modest, hinting at—rather than revealing—her curves. But the white piqué was a perfect foil for her dark hair and eyes. She wore a delicate gold chain at her neck, and his eyes lingered for a moment on the spot where it rested against the creamy skin at the edge of her collarbone.

Eric swallowed past the sudden lump in his throat, fighting a swift—and disconcerting—surge of panic. Until this moment he'd felt somehow insulated from Kate's beauty, gentle manner and earnest efforts to do the right thing for her daughter. He'd admired her, but he'd felt in control and able to keep a safe emotional distance. Suddenly he didn't feel at all in control. Or safe. Or distant.

But that wasn't *her* problem, he reminded himself. He'd just have to deal with his own surprising reaction later. Right now he needed to make her relax. And that would be no small chore, he realized. The pulsating shimmer of her gold chain clearly suggested accelerated respiration, indicating that she was as nervous about this setup as he suddenly was. Not a good sign.

Deliberately he tipped his lips up into a smile, and when he spoke his voice was warm and friendly—but purposely not *too* friendly. "Hello, Kate. I..."

"Hi, Dr. Eric." Sarah burst into the room, dragging her sweater by one sleeve.

He grinned at Kate as Sarah's exuberant entrance dissipated the tension in the room, then he squatted down beside his small patient and touched her nose.

"Hello, Sarah. Are you still having those tummyaches?"

"No. They're all gone. You must be a very good doctor."

He chuckled. "I think maybe Dr. Anna can take the credit for your cure."

Sarah gave him a puzzled look. "Is Aunt Anna a doctor, too?"

He smiled. "In some ways. She always used to make me feel better after I fell off my bike and scraped my knees."

"I like her," Sarah declared.

"So do I."

"We're going to make cookies tonight and watch *Mary Poppins*."

"Now that sounds like fun."

"You can come, too," Sarah offered.

"I'd like to. But I promised my friend I'd come to his party. Maybe we can watch a movie together sometime, though."

"Can Mommy watch, too?"

Eric glanced up at Kate apologetically, realizing he'd put her in an awkward position. "Sure. If she wants to."

"Oh, Mommy likes movies. Don't you, Mommy?"

Kate didn't answer. Instead, she picked up her purse. "Shouldn't we be leaving? I promised Sarah I wouldn't be gone too long, and it's getting late."

He rose slowly, aware that she was laying out the ground rules for tonight. Clearly, it was going to be a short evening. Still, it was better than nothing, he consoled himself. Even a couple of hours in the company of adults, where she could laugh and relax, might help chase the haunted look from her eyes.

"Yes, we should."

As he turned toward the door the phone rang, and Kate hesitated. Then she sighed. "I'd better get it. It will only take a minute."

"No rush."

Although Sarah's chatter kept him occupied during Kate's absence, Eric took the opportunity to glance around her modest apartment. There was a small living room, a tiny kitchenette with a counter that served as a dining table, and—judging by the three doors opening off the short hallway—apparently two bedrooms and a bath. The unit was barely large enough for two people, let alone three, he concluded with a frown. How had they managed in such a confined space when her mother was alive?

Apparently there'd been no choice. His mother had mentioned Kate's comment about her finances being depleted, and this tiny, older apartment was eloquent testimony to a tight budget. Yet she'd made it a home, he realized, noting with appreciation the warm touches that gave the rooms a comfortable, inviting feel. One of Sarah's drawings had been framed and hung on the wall. A cross-stitched pillow rested on the couch. Green plants flourished in a wicker stand by the window. And several family photos were prominently displayed.

His eyes lingered on the photo on top of the television. Kate was holding a tiny baby and a man sat next to her, on the edge of a couch, his arm protectively around her shoulders. Jack. Eric recognized him from the night of the accident. And on the opposite wall hung a wedding picture in which Kate and Jack were slightly younger—and obviously very much in love.

"That's my daddy," Sarah declared, noting the direction of Eric's gaze.

He smiled down at her. "That's what I thought. He looks very nice."

Sarah turned to study the picture gravely. "Mommy says he was. She says he loved me very much." She transferred her gaze to the photo on the TV. "That's me in that picture, when I was a baby. That's my daddy, too. I don't remember him, though. He went to heaven right after I was born."

Eric felt his throat tighten, but before he could respond Kate spoke from the hallway.

"I'm sorry for the delay. We can go now."

He looked up, and the raw pain in her eyes tugged at his heart.

"Did you know my daddy?" Sarah asked Eric, oblivious to Kate's distress.

With an effort he withdrew his gaze from Kate's and glanced back down at Sarah. "No. I wish I had," he said gently.

"So do I. Then you could tell me what he was like. Mommy tells me stories about him, but sometimes she cries and it makes me sad."

"Sarah! That's enough about Daddy!" Kate admonished, her face flushed. When she saw Sarah's startled gaze, her eyes filled with dismay and she gentled her tone. "You don't want to keep Aunt Anna waiting, do you? She's probably all ready to make those cookies."

A slightly subdued Sarah walked to the door. "We were waiting for *you*, Mommy," she pointed out in a hurt voice that only made Kate feel worse.

Sarah talked nonstop to Eric during the short drive, and when they dropped her off, Anna wished them a pleasant evening and told them not to hurry. "We'll have lots of fun, won't we, Sarah?"

The little girl nodded vigorously, and Kate bent down beside her.

"You be a good girl, now. And Mommy will be back soon." Her voice sounded artificially bright, and the slight, almost-unnoticeable catch at the end tugged at Eric's heart.

"Okay."

It was Kate who seemed reluctant to part, he noted. Sarah seemed perfectly happy to spend the evening with his mother. Kate confirmed his impression as they drove away.

"You know, this is the first time I've ever left her with a sitter, except for day care," she admitted, her voice slightly unsteady.

"She'll be fine," he reassured her. "She and Mom get along famously."

"I know. And I'm grateful. But I feel guilty for leaving her with someone when I don't have to."

"You need a life, too, Kate," he gently pointed out. "Apart from Sarah. When was the last time you went out socially?" He caught her surprised glance out of the corner of his eye and turned to her apologetically. "Sorry. That's none of my business. But I have the impression you don't get out much, other than to your job. That's not healthy."

"Is that your professional opinion?"

"I'm not a psychiatrist. But balance is important to a healthy lifestyle."

"From what your mother has told me, it sounds like maybe you need to take your own advice."

He grimaced. "Touché. I do spend a lot of hours at work. But I also take time occasionally to socialize. Like tonight."

Kate turned to stare out the front windshield. "I *want* to be with Sarah, Eric. It's not a chore. Besides, I don't know that many people here. We lived in Cincinnati until a few months before Sarah was born. When we first moved to St. Louis we were too busy fixing up our house to socialize. And afterward... Well, I had no time to make friends. I was with Jack every minute I could spare. Since he died, I simply haven't had the interest or the energy to meet people. Besides, Sarah is all I need."

"Have you ever thought that maybe *she* needs more?" he suggested carefully.

Kate frowned. "Like what?"

"Friends her own age. Is she involved in any activities with other children?"

Kate stiffened. "There aren't many children in our apartment complex. And there's nowhere for her to play unless I take her to the park down the street. We get along, Eric. It's not ideal, but then, nothing is."

Eric could sense Kate's tension in her defensive posture. Not a good way to start their evening, he realized. It was time to back off.

"I didn't mean to be critical, Kate. You're right. Nothing is ideal. And your social life is none of my business. But I appreciate your willingness to help me out tonight. You'll like Frank and Mary. And maybe we'll both have some fun."

There was that word again. "Fun." It seemed so

foreign, so distant. She could hardly remember what it was like to indulge in pure, carefree fun with other adults. And she didn't expect her memory to be jogged tonight.

But much to her surprise, it was.

Kate wasn't sure at exactly what point she began to relax and enjoy herself. Maybe it was when Frank told the hilarious story about how he and his wife met after Mary ran into his car. Or maybe it was when Mary learned that she and Kate liked the same author, then loaned her the woman's latest book, even though Kate protested that she never had time to read anymore. "Make time," Mary said, and extracted a promise that Kate would call her to talk about the book after she finished it. Or maybe it was when she got coaxed into a game of lawn darts, and much to everyone's surprise—including her own—proved that she had an incredibly accurate aim by trouncing one challenger after another.

All Kate knew was that suddenly she found herself laughing—and relaxing. It took her by surprise, but it also felt good. So good, in fact, that for a moment it made her eyes sting as she recalled the fun and laughter that had once been part of her normal, everyday existence. Nothing had been "normal" in her life for years, but tonight reminded her of what she had once had—and so often had taken for granted. This brief reprieve from the deep-seated sadness that had shrouded her existence for so long was like a life vest thrown to one adrift, and she clung to it greedily. Even if it only lasted tonight, she thought, it gave her a precious moment in the sunlight after years of darkness.

As Kate won her fourth round of lawn darts, Frank

held up his hands in defeat. "That's it. I give up. I'm not a glutton for punishment. I duly declare Kate the Queen of Lawn Darts. And now I think it's time to move on to something more important. Let's eat."

Mary poked him in the ribs good-naturedly. "Is that all you ever think about? Food?"

He glanced down at her five-months-pregnant girth and grinned. "Obviously not."

She blushed and rolled her eyes. "I'm not going to touch that one with a ten-foot pole," she declared. "Let's eat."

"Isn't that what I just said?" he teased.

Kate watched their affectionate interplay with both amusement and envy. She and Jack had once shared that kind of closeness, where a look spoke volumes and a simple touch could unite two hearts. Even after all these years, whenever she saw a couple communicating in that special nonverbal way reserved for those deeply in love, her heart ached with the realization that for her those golden days were gone forever.

Eric saw the sudden melancholy sweep over Kate's face, and he frowned. He'd been keenly attuned to the nuances in her mood all evening, watching with pleasure as her initial uncertainty and subdued demeanor gave way to tentative smiles and then relaxed interaction. Eric was taken aback the first time he heard her musical laugh, then entranced by it. He was captivated when her eyes occasionally sparkled with delight. And he was charmed by her unaffected beauty and unconscious grace. It had been an incredible transformation—and he intended to do everything he could to sustain it.

"Did I hear someone say food?" he asked, coming up quickly behind her.

Mary gave him a rueful grin. "You men are all alike."

"Well, I certainly hope so," her husband countered with a wink. "Come on, we need to lead off or no one will eat." He took her arm and led her purposefully toward the buffet table.

Eric nodded toward the food line. "Shall we?"

Kate stepped forward, and he dropped his hand lightly to her waist, guiding her toward the serving table with a slight pressure in the small of her back. His touch startled her at first. She knew it was an impersonal gesture, born more of good manners than attraction, yet it sent an odd tingle racing along her spine. It had been a long time since she'd been touched like this. She'd almost forgotten the sense of protection it gave her—and how good it felt. She'd missed these simple little gestures, she realized with a pang. They went a long way toward making a person feel cared for. Yet she'd never recognized their importance until they were absent. And by then it was too late to experience again and savor those special, everyday moments that truly defined a relationship.

Eric heard her small sigh and looked at her with concern as he picked up two plates. "Is something wrong?"

She summoned a smile, but it was edged with sadness. "I was just remembering that old cliché, about how you never really appreciate something until it's gone." Her gaze strayed to Frank and Mary, who were holding hands as they carried their plates to a table. "They're a really nice couple."

Eric followed her gaze, then handed her a plate. "Yes, they are. It renews your faith in romance to see two people who are obviously in love."

They filled their plates in silence, and when they reached the end of the line he led the way toward a secluded table. Kate hesitated and glanced back toward the group.

"Shouldn't we mingle?"

"We've been doing that all night. Don't worry. Frank won't take offense." He deposited his plate on a table for two under a rose arbor and held out her chair. "This is a perfect spot for dinner, don't you think?"

Kate couldn't argue with that. It reminded her of an old-fashioned garden—the kind she'd once planned to have. Nowadays she had to content herself with a few ferns and African violets tucked into sunny corners of her apartment. She couldn't even give Sarah a proper yard to play in, she thought dispiritedly, her gaze drifting back to Frank and Mary. Their child would be blessed with two loving parents and plenty of room to stretch his or her legs—and wings, she thought wistfully.

As Eric sat down, one look at Kate's face made him realize that there was no way he could salvage her lighthearted mood. And maybe he shouldn't even try. Maybe she needed to talk about the things that had made the light in her eyes flicker and die.

"I have a feeling that watching Frank and Mary reminds you of your own marriage," he remarked quietly.

She looked at him in surprise, then gazed unseeingly at her plate as she toyed with her food. At first he wasn't sure she was going to respond. But a moment later she spoke.

"In some ways," she acknowledged softly, "Jack and I weren't as outgoing, but we had that same kind of special bond. I guess once you've experienced it, you just recognize it in others. Seeing Frank and Mary together makes me remember what I once had."

"I'm sorry about how things turned out, Kate. I guess the only consolation is that at least you had that special bond once."

She glanced at him. He was staring at his own plate now, apparently lost for a moment in his own memories. He seemed sad, and there was disillusion—and regret—in his eyes. Obviously she wasn't the only one with grief in her past, Kate realized with a sharp pang. Apparently Eric had not only gone through a painful divorce, but a painful marriage as well, devoid of the kind of love all young couples dream of. In some ways, perhaps the death of that dream was worse than living the dream and then losing it, she reflected. At least she had happy memories. His seemed depressing at best.

"Now it's my turn to say I'm sorry." She watched as, with an effort, he pulled himself back to the present.

He shrugged. "I survived—with the help of my family and my faith."

She looked down. "I had the family part, anyway."

Eric frowned. "No faith?"

"Not anymore."

"But Mom said that Sarah mentioned Sunday school."

"My mother used to take her. I feel badly that I haven't followed through, but my heart's not in it."

"What happened?"

She played with the edge of her napkin. "Jack and I went to church regularly. I used to think God really listened when we prayed," she said haltingly.

"And now?"

"Let's just say I haven't seen much evidence that He does. I prayed when Jack was injured. Pleaded, actually. And bargained. And begged. I put my trust in God's hands, always believing He'd come through for me. But He didn't. So I figured, what's the use? If God wasn't listening to me, why keep talking? That's when I stopped praying. And going to church. Mom picked up the slack with Sarah, but I've kind of dropped the ball since she...since she died. I feel guilty about it, but I just can't go back yet. Maybe I never will. I'm still too angry at God."

"You know, there's a simple fix for the guilt about Sarah, at least."

She gazed at him curiously. "There is?"

"Yes. Mom and I go to church every Sunday. We'd be more than happy to take her with us."

Kate looked at him in surprise, then frowned. "But you've both done so much for me already. It just doesn't seem right."

"Well, then, think of it this way. We'd actually be doing this for Sarah."

She conceded his point with a slight lift of her shoulders. "I can't argue with that. Are you really sure you wouldn't mind?"

"Absolutely. We'll start tomorrow. You'd be welcome to join us anytime."

"I'll keep that in mind."

"It really might help, you know," he pressed gently. "It was a lifesaver for me. We have a wonderful minister. He's helped me through some pretty rough times.''

Kate didn't want to discuss the state of her soul with anyone. She had too many conflicting emotions about her faith, too many unanswered questions. But she *would* like to know more about what had happened to turn Eric so completely off marriage. So far, he'd asked most of the questions. It seemed only fair that she return the favor.

"I take it your marriage wasn't exactly...memorable," she ventured.

An expression of pain seared across his eyes, like the white-hot flash of fireworks—brief but intense. "Oh, it was memorable, all right." Though she saw he tried to mask it, the bitterness in his tone was unmistakable.

"Is it something you can talk about? Sometimes that helps. And I used to be a good listener. I'm a little out of practice, but I can give it a try."

Even as she spoke the words, Kate was startled by their truthfulness. For the last few years she had been so focused on her own pain that she'd been oblivious to the pain of others. In one blinding moment of revelation, she realized that she had slipped, without even being aware of it, into self-pity and self-absorption. It was a disturbing insight. One of the things Jack had loved about her was her openness to others and her ability to empathize. He would hardly have recognized her now, she conceded. Since his death she'd closed herself off to everyone and everything except Sarah, her mother and her sister. And it had been an effective coping mechanism, insulating her with a numbness that made the pain in her life bearable.

But living the rest of her life in darkness and grief wasn't going to bring Jack back, she acknowledged sadly. Somehow she had to find her way back to beauty and joy and hope, because suddenly she knew she couldn't go on marking the days instead of living them. It wasn't fair to her, or to Sarah—or to the memory of Jack, who had loved life intensely and lived each day with passion and appreciation, fully embracing all the blessings the Lord had bestowed on him.

But Kate had no idea how to begin the rebuilding process. It seemed like such a daunting task. Maybe listening to Eric, as he had listened to her, would be a way to start connecting with people again.

When her gaze linked with his, she found him watching her intently and she shifted uncomfortably. Was he angry that she'd turned the tables and asked about *his* private life? she wondered anxiously. She hadn't meant to offend him. "Listen, I didn't mean to pry, Eric. I'm sorry."

"It's not that," he assured her quickly. "It's just that you— I don't know, you had a funny look on your face for a minute."

"Did I?" His perceptiveness surprised—and slightly unnerved—her. "I guess I was wondering if maybe I'd overstepped my bounds, asking about your marriage," she hedged, reluctant to reveal the personal insight that had just flashed through her mind. "It's just that talking to you about Jack and my faith helped tonight. I thought maybe it might help you to talk, too. But I understand if you'd rather not."

He looked at her for a moment before he spoke, as if assessing whether her interest was real or just polite. "Actually, I haven't talked much about it to anyone.

Except my minister. Maybe because there isn't a whole lot to say. And because it still hurts after all these years. And because it's hard to admit failure," he confessed candidly. "But I'll give you the highlights—or lowlights, depending on your perspective—if you're really interested."

"I am."

He gave a slight nod. "Cindy and I met when I was in medical school," he began. "She was blond and beautiful, carefree and fun, always ready for the next adventure. I was the serious, studious type and it was exciting just to be with her. I never knew what she'd do next. All I knew was that she added a whole new dimension to my life. As different as we were, something clicked between us and I proposed a year after we met. We got married a few months later."

"Sounds like a promising beginning," Kate ventured.

"Yeah. Except things just went downhill from there. She didn't like my choice of specialty, and she grew to resent the intrusion of my career on our personal lives. We both changed through the years—or maybe we just became more of what we'd always been. In any case, the differences we once found so appealing gradually became irritating and hurtful. In the end, we were barely speaking."

He paused and looked down at his iced tea. The drops of condensation on his glass reminded him of tears, and he suddenly felt sad. "To be honest, I don't think either of us was blameless in the breakup, but I feel most responsible," he said heavily. "Cindy was right about my career—it takes an inordinate amount of my time. And it was a self-perpetuating kind of thing. As our marriage disintegrated, I spent even more time in the office and at the hospital, which only made matters worse. I don't know.... Maybe she would have been more tolerant of my schedule if I'd been doing heart transplants or something."

Kate frowned. "What do you mean?"

"Cindy wanted me to be a surgeon. That's considered one of the more 'glamorous' specialties. And when we got married, I thought I wanted to do that, too. But eventually I realized that I didn't enjoy practicing medicine in that sterile environment. I wanted to interact with people. And I love kids. Pediatrics was a natural fit for me. But Cindy hated it. It didn't have enough prestige. She was bitterly disappointed in my choice—and in me. Over time, our relationship grew strained and distant, and in the end it just fell apart." Eric didn't tell Kate about the final hurt—the reason he'd finally agreed to the divorce. Even now, five years later, it made him feel physically ill to think about it.

Impulsively Kate reached out and touched his hand. "I'm sorry, Eric."

Startled, he dropped his gaze to her slender fingers lightly resting on his sun-browned hand. It was funny. He couldn't remember a single time during his entire relationship with Cindy when she'd touched him in quite this way, with such heartfelt empathy and simple human caring. His throat tightened, and he swallowed with difficulty.

"So am I," he admitted, his voice suddenly husky. "I always believed marriage was forever, that if things got rough you worked them out. But by the time I brought up the idea of counseling, it was too late. Cindy had already given up. She finally asked for a divorce, and under the circumstances I agreed. But in my heart I still feel married. I spoke those vows in the sight of God, and I can't forget them as easily as she did.''

''What do you mean?''

''She remarried a few months after the divorce became final. She and her new husband live in Denver. It's not that I'm judging her, Kate. I leave that to God. But it wasn't the right thing for me.''

''So that's what your mother meant when she said she'd better take this opportunity to play grandmother,'' Kate mused aloud.

Eric looked surprised. ''She told you that?''

''Yes. The day I met her.''

''Well, maybe my message is finally sinking in. But I know she's disappointed. As the only child, I was her one hope for grandchildren,'' he said ruefully.

''Hey, hey, hey! This conversation looks way too heavy,'' Frank interrupted with a grin. ''Time to liven things up a little. Okay, Kate, one more round of lawn darts. I feel renewed after that meal.''

Kate smiled and glanced at her watch. ''I really need to get home,'' she protested.

''Eric, convince her.''

Eric shrugged. ''He'll be a bear to work with if he doesn't get a chance to redeem himself.''

Kate laughed. ''Okay. One more round.''

Fifteen minutes later, after she had once more soundly beaten her host, she and Eric said their goodbyes.

''He'll never live this down, you know,'' Eric told her with a chuckle as he escorted her to his car, his hand again placed possessively in the small of her back.

"Oh, people will forget," she replied with a smile.

"I won't," he declared smugly.

"Eric! You aren't going to use this against him, are you?"

"You'd better believe it," he asserted promptly, grinning as he opened her door. "What are friends for?"

Kate shook her head and slid in. A moment later he took his place behind the wheel. "You know, he's going to be sorry I came tonight," she predicted.

Eric smiled. "Maybe so. But do you know something, Kate?" At the odd note in his voice she turned to look at him. "I'm not. I had a really good time."

At his words, a feeling of warmth and happiness washed over her like a healing balm. "So did I," she admitted quietly. "Thanks for asking me."

"It was my pleasure." As he pulled away from the curb, he glanced over at her. "Maybe we can do it again sometime."

Again? Kate wasn't sure that was wise. It wasn't that she found Eric's company lacking. He was a great conversationalist, an empathetic listener, intelligent, well-read—not to mention incredibly handsome. She liked him. A lot. And therein lay the problem. She liked him *too* much. While she might have reached a turning point in her life tonight, she wasn't ready to deal with relationships—at least, not the male/female variety. And that included Eric—despite the fact that he wasn't even in the market for romance.

Like Eric, Kate believed in that "till death us do part" vow. Even though she was no longer bound by it, in her heart she still felt married. Yet being with Eric tonight had awakened feelings long suppressed— and best left undisturbed, she decided firmly. Though her reactions had been subtle, they spelled danger. Intuitively she knew that Eric Carlson's very presence could disrupt her life by raising questions she wasn't yet ready to address and forcing her to examine issues she wasn't prepared to face.

She turned and gazed out into the night with a troubled frown, oblivious to the passing scenery. Even her mild reaction—or maybe *attraction* was a better word, she admitted honestly—to Eric tonight made her feel guilty; as if she were somehow betraying the love she and Jack had shared. It was *not* a good feeling. And the best way to keep it from happening again was to stay away from the disturbing man beside her.

It was as simple as that.

Chapter Four

Okay, maybe it wasn't quite *that* simple, Kate conceded the next morning as she waited for Eric to pick Sarah up for church. Their paths were going to cross every Sunday at this rate unless she decided to take Sarah to services herself. And that wasn't likely to happen anytime in the near future. So she'd just have to get used to seeing him once a week and maintain a polite distance.

Except that would be easier said than done, she acknowledged with a sigh. There was just something about him that drew her. Maybe it was his eyes, she mused. They were wonderful eyes. Understanding. Warm. Caring. Compelling. She'd never seen eyes quite so intensely blue before—nor so insightful. When he gazed at her she felt he could almost see into her soul.

Strangely enough, that didn't bother her, even though she'd always been a very private person. Maybe because—stranger still—she felt as if they weren't just recent acquaintances, but old friends. Which made no sense. For all practical purposes, they'd met less than two weeks ago. Nevertheless, the feeling of familiarity persisted. It was disconcerting—yet somehow oddly comforting.

The doorbell rang, and Sarah dashed to answer it. Kate followed more slowly, grateful that Eric's attention was distracted by his young greeter long enough for her to take a quick inventory—and then struggle to regain control of a breathing pattern that suddenly went haywire as she stared at him.

Kate had always known that Eric was a handsome man. He had classic Nordic good looks, and in a different age might have stood at the helm of a questing ship. Yet his gentle manner and kindheartedness were at odds with those Viking images of old. It seemed he had inherited the best of both worlds—ancient athletic virility and modern male sensibilities. It was a stunning—and extremely appealing—combination. And never had it come across more clearly than today. In a light-gray summer suit that emphasized his lean, muscular frame, and a crisp white shirt and dark blue, patterned tie, he was by far the most attractive man Kate had seen in a long time. Or maybe he was just the first one she'd *noticed* in a long time, she acknowledged with a frown.

He chose that moment to look up, and his smile of greeting faded when he saw her troubled expression. "Everything okay?"

She forced the corners of her mouth to lift and closed the distance between them. "Fine."

"Not having second thoughts?"

"No, of course not."

He studied her for a moment with those discerning eyes, as if debating whether to pursue the subject. Much to her relief, he let it rest. "We usually go to breakfast after services. Would you like us to swing by and pick you up? Make it a foursome?"

"Can we, Mommy?" Sarah asked eagerly. "I could get pancakes. I like pancakes," she told Eric.

He grinned. "So do I." He transferred his gaze back to Kate, and his expression softened. Or was it only her imagination? she wondered. "How about it, Kate?"

"I appreciate the offer, Eric, but your mom told me that's your special time together. We wouldn't want to intrude."

"Actually, it was her idea. But I had the same thought. She just brought it up first," he said with an engaging grin.

"Oh. Well, maybe another time. I really hadn't planned on going out at all today. I need to work on some lesson plans."

"Now what's that old saying? 'All work and no play makes Jack a—'" At the sudden pallor of Kate's face, Eric stopped short, his jaw tightening in self-reproach. Of all the stupid remarks! "Kate, I'm sorry. I just didn't think."

"It's...it's all right," she assured him shakily. "It's just that— Well, that saying was Jack's motto. He was a great believer in keeping things in proper perspective. He always made sure we took time for fun, and he never forgot to smell the flowers along the way."

"I have a feeling I would have liked him," Eric said quietly.

She summoned up a sad smile. "I think you might be right."

"Are we going now?" Sarah asked impatiently.

With an effort, Eric released Kate's gaze and smiled down at the little girl. "I don't think I've ever seen anyone quite so anxious to go to church," he teased. "God will be very happy."

"I just want to show Aunt Anna my new dress. Mommy bought it for me this summer and we were saving it for a special occasion."

Kate liked the deep, rich sound of the chuckle that rumbled out of Eric's chest. "Well, we won't tell God that's the reason you want to hurry. We wouldn't want to hurt His feelings."

"I want to go to church, too," Sarah assured him. "I like the singing."

"I'll walk out to the car with you," Kate said. "I'd like to say hello to Anna."

The two women exchanged a few words while Eric settled Sarah in the back seat, then he rejoined them.

"You're sure you won't come to breakfast, Kate?" Anna asked.

"Maybe another time. But thank you."

"I'll see you back to your door," Eric told her.

She looked at him in surprise. "That's really not necessary."

"Yes, it is. I have something I want to ask you."

He fell into step beside her, and she looked up at him curiously. "Is there a problem?"

He smiled ruefully. "That depends on how you look at it, I guess. I have another favor to ask, and I'd like you to consider it while we're at church." He reached up and adjusted his tie, and Kate would have sworn he was nervous. "In addition to my job, I'm on the board of several local health-related organizations. As Mom told you, I have a tendency to slightly overextend myself," he admitted wryly.

She smiled. "I think her exact words were that it's harder for you to say no to a good cause than for a gopher to stop digging holes."

He chuckled, and a pleasing crinkle of lines appeared at the corners of his eyes. "That sounds like Mom. Anyway, next Saturday night there's a black-tie dinner dance that's the culmination of the annual fund-raising drive for one of the organizations. Usually I try to avoid these things, but I can't get out of this one. I could go alone, but to be honest, it always feels a little awkward." They reached her door, and he turned toward her. "So I wondered if you might go with me. Will you think about it while we're at church, Kate?"

She gazed up into his clear blue eyes, and for a moment she felt as if she were basking in the warmth of the summer sun under a cloudless sky. It was a good feeling—one that had been absent from her life for a long time. But it also made her nervous. She dropped her gaze, unsure how to answer. Something told her she should say no immediately. But she didn't want to hurt Eric's feelings. He had gone out of his way to be kind to her and Sarah. And besides, she had enjoyed their time together the evening before.

"Kate?"

She looked back up at him, took a deep breath and suddenly decided to follow her heart. "All right, Eric. I'll think about it," she agreed.

She was rewarded with a smile that lit up his face and made his eyes glow. A person could get lost in those eyes, she thought, mesmerized by their warmth. "Thanks, Kate. And don't work too hard while we're gone."

"N-no, I won't. See you later," she said breathlessly, then quickly slipped inside.

For a long time after he left, Kate stood with her back braced against the front door, trying to reconcile her conflicting emotions. She felt more alive than she had in years—but she was also troubled. And she knew why. Her gaze strayed to her wedding picture, and she tenderly traced the contours of Jack's dear, familiar face. Her love for him was as strong now as it had been on that day nearly eleven years before when they'd been joined as man and wife. It had not diminished one iota.

But other things had, she thought sadly, tears welling in her eyes. Certain images and sensory memories were slowly slipping away, despite her desperate efforts to hold on to them. The funny, dismayed face Jack always made whenever she served carrots. The deep timbre of his voice during their intimate moments. The feel of his freshly-shaved skin beneath her fingertips. The distinctive, woodsy scent of his after-shave. The way he always tilted his head as he cut the grass.

All of those things were fading, like an old photograph in which all that remained were vague outlines of images that had once been sharp and clear and vibrant. Soon she would only be able to remember the *fact* that those things had once been special, not the unique qualities that made them so. She was losing Jack, bit by bit, day by day, and there was nothing she could do to stop it. The sense of distance and the ebbing of memories had accelerated in the last few months, she realized, and it left her with a sick, hollow, helpless feeling that seemed destined to plague her well into the foreseeable future.

And then, out of the blue, Eric Carlson had stepped into her life. With him, she didn't feel as hopeless and depressed. In fact, he made her feel things she'd never expected to feel again—attractive, womanly, cared for. He'd awakened in her needs that she had suppressed for five long years; needs she'd thought were forever locked within the cold recesses of her heart. Slowly, under the warmth of his gaze, those needs were beginning to thaw. And that scared her. After all, she was a lonely widow. He was a handsome divorced man. Even if the widow was still in love with her husband and the divorced man still felt married, it just didn't seem like a safe combination.

Kate wasn't sure what to do. But she knew whom to call for advice. And she intended to place that call just as soon as she poured herself a cup of coffee.

"Kate? What's wrong? I thought it was my turn to call *you* this Sunday."

"Nothing's wrong, Amy. I didn't mean to scare you," she apologized quickly, dismayed by the alarm in her sister's voice. "I just had some free time and thought I'd call you first, that's all."

"Thank God! I didn't mean to overreact, but—"

"That's okay. You have good reason. My unexpected phone calls haven't always been exactly uplifting."

"Yeah, well, hopefully those days are over. So what's the occasion? It's not my birthday or anything. How come you're springing for this Sunday's call?"

"Can't I be generous once in a while?"

"Look, neither of us can afford to be generous. Why don't I call you back tonight, as usual? It *is* my turn. Every other week, remember?"

"I remember. But I just wanted to talk. Unless... Are you getting ready for church?"

"Nope. Cal pulled a midnight shift at the park last night and is sleeping in. We're going to the second service. So I've got the time. But you haven't got the money."

"Will you quit with the money thing?"

"I'd like to. But neither of us can afford to treat money lightly—no pun intended. Just consider the facts. You're a single working mother with huge medical debts. I have three kids, my husband makes his living dressed like Smokey the Bear, we live in a log cabin and I make quilts to keep the wolf from the door. Case closed."

That wasn't quite the whole story, but Kate let it pass with a smile. "You forgot one thing."

"What?"

"You love every minute of your life."

Kate heard her sister's contented sigh. "Yeah, I do. But we'll never have money to spare. I'm always sorry we couldn't do more to help you, Kate."

"You did the most important thing, Amy. You were there. You and Mom. That was worth more than gold."

"Still, gold comes in handy sometimes. Speaking of which—how are you doing with the bills?"

"Okay. I pay off a little every month. I figure at this rate I'll be free and clear about the time I'm ready to retire." She tried for a light tone, but didn't quite pull it off.

"You know, Kate, sometimes I think that... Well, I've never said this before, but...but since things turned out the way they did, it almost would have been better if—well—if Jack hadn't..." Amy's voice trailed off.

"I've thought about that, too," Kate admitted slowly. "But at the time I was just grateful he survived the accident." She paused and took a deep breath, determined not to dwell on what might have been. She needed Amy's advice about the future, not about the past. "Actually, in a roundabout way, that's one of the reasons I called today. You'll never believe this coincidence, but the doctor who saved Eric's life at the accident scene is Sarah's new pediatrician."

"No kidding? That's weird! Did he recognize you?"

"Uh-huh. Even before I recognized him. As a matter of fact, his mother is watching Sarah for me while I teach."

"How in the world did you arrange that?"

"I didn't. He did." Sarah explained, ending with Eric's offer to take Sarah to church each Sunday.

"Wow! I doubt whether my pediatrician, nice as she is, would ever take such a personal interest in *my* kids," Amy commented, clearly impressed.

"I've been really lucky," Kate acknowledged. "But I do have a sort of...dilemma."

"So tell me about it."

In halting phrases, Kate told Amy about Eric's marital situation, their evening together and his second invitation.

"So I honestly don't know what to do," she admitted at the end.

As usual, Amy honed right in on the key question. "Well, do you *want* to go?"

Kate frowned. "I—I think so. I like him, and we had a really good time. But when I'm with him I...I feel things I haven't felt in a long time. And then I feel guilty."

"You have nothing to feel guilty about," Amy declared firmly. "You're a healthy young woman who's been living in an emotional cave for way too long. Why shouldn't you go out and have a good time?"

"You know why."

"Because of Jack."

"I still love him, Amy. I still feel married. It just doesn't seem right, somehow, to go out with another man. Even one who's not interested in romance."

There was silence for a brief moment before Amy spoke. "Can I tell you something, Kate?"

"Why do I have the feeling you will anyway, even if I say no?"

"Because you know me too well," Amy replied pertly. Then her voice grew more serious. "Look, I'll just say this straight out, okay? I know you loved Jack. And I know why. He was a great guy. We *all* loved him. And we all still miss him. We always will. As his wife, I know you feel the loss more intensely than any of us can even imagine. When I think of life without Cal... Well, it makes me understand in a very small way the pain you've had to deal with. But Jack wouldn't want you to go through the rest of your life without ever really living again, Kate. And part of living is loving. I know you have Sarah. But I'm not talking about that kind of love. You're the kind of woman who blossoms when she's loved by the right man. That's not to say you're not strong or capable or independent. You're all of those things, and you've

proved it over and over again these past five years. But
don't close yourself off to life—and love—because of
a misplaced sense of obligation or guilt. Jack wouldn't
want that, and deep in your heart you know that. Nothing can ever take away the memory of the special love
you two shared. That's yours forever. But maybe it's
time to start making some new memories."

For a long moment there was silence. Sometimes
Kate felt that Amy, though two years younger, was
really the older of the two. She was so solid, so
grounded, so blessed with common sense and the ability to quickly analyze a situation and offer valuable
insight. People didn't always like what Amy said. But
they could rarely deny the truth of her words.

"Kate?" Amy said worriedly. "Are you still there?
Look, I'm sorry if I overstepped, but—"

"It's okay," Kate interrupted. "Actually, I think
you're right in a lot of ways. It's just that... Well, it's
not easy to let go."

"I know, hon," Amy murmured sympathetically.
"But you're going to have to let go before you can
really get on with your life."

Kate played with the phone cord. "Jack's kind of
slipping away anyway, you know?" Her voice broke
on the last word.

"Oh, Kate, I wish I was there right now to give you
a hug!"

"Yeah, so do I."

"You know, maybe this slipping away is Jack's—
and the Lord's—way of telling you it's time to move
on."

"Maybe. But... I don't know. I guess I'm just
scared, Amy."

"That's okay. That's normal. But don't let fear stop you. It's like that old saying about ships. They may be safe in the harbor, but that's not what they're built for. I think it's time for you to set sail, Kate."

"How come you always know the right thing to say?" Kate asked, smiling mistily as she swiped at her eyes.

Amy chuckled. "My kids wouldn't agree with that."

"They will when they get older. Listen, thanks, okay? I feel a lot better."

"So are you going with Eric?"

"I guess so. But don't start getting any romantic ideas. I told you, he's not in the market."

"That's okay. At least he'll get you back into circulation, introduce you to some new people. That's a start. And I'll want a full report next Sunday. Except *I'll* call *you.* Agreed?"

"Agreed."

"So, you've been holding out on your old pal all this time."

Eric glanced up from the chart he was reading. Frank was lounging against the door of his office, arms folded, one ankle crossed over the other, his accusatory tone tempered by the twinkle in his eyes.

"What's that supposed to mean?" As if he didn't know. He'd been waiting all afternoon for Frank to pounce and demand details about Eric's date.

"You know very well what I mean. Here I think you're a miserable, lonely, driven man desperately in need of female companionship and then you show up with a babe like Kate. Boy, you had me fooled! Where have you been hiding her all this time?"

"I haven't been 'hiding' her anywhere. And I'm not sure she'd appreciate the term 'babe,' even though I know you mean it in an entirely flattering way. How about if we just refer to her as the Queen of Lawn Darts?"

Frank grimaced. "Ouch! You would have to bring that up. I just had an off night. So…" He ambled over and perched on the edge of Eric's desk, not about to be distracted. "Tell me everything. Where did you meet this goddess? And how serious are you two?"

"We're just friends, Frank. That's it."

His partner gave a skeptical snort. "Yeah. Like Ma Barker was just a sweet old lady."

"I'm serious."

"You expect me to buy that after the way you were looking at her all night?"

Eric sent him a startled look. "What do you mean?"

"Oh, come on, man. You hung on her every word. You made it a point to keep tabs on her whenever you were apart—which wasn't often. And you have that look in your eye."

"What look?"

"Smitten. Enamored. Head over heels. Is that descriptive enough?"

Eric frowned. "You're crazy."

"Uh-uh. I know that look. Had it once myself. Still do sometimes, in fact."

"Well, with all due respect to your powers of perception, you're way off base this time, pal."

Frank tilted his head and considered his friend thoughtfully for a moment. Then he grinned and stood. "Good try. But no sale. However, I get the message— butt out. Okay, that's fine, don't bare your soul to me, even though I'm your best friend in the world. I can read a No Trespassing sign when I see one." He ambled to the door and disappeared into the hall, but a moment later he stuck his head back inside and grinned. "But I don't pay any attention to signs. I'll wear you down eventually, you know. In the meantime, don't worry, buddy. Your secret's safe with me."

Eric stared at the doorway, then frowned and leaned back in his chair, absently playing with his pen. Frank might be a bit outspoken and on the boisterous side, but his powers of perception were keen. Usually he nailed a person's personality within five minutes of meeting him or her. He was even more intuitive about friends and associates. Sometimes it was almost scary.

Like right now.

Eric's frown deepened. Was Frank overreacting? Or had he seen something Eric had overlooked? There was no question that he liked Kate. And he *had* carried a memory of her in his mind for more than five years— but only because he'd been struck by her beauty and obvious love for her husband. Her transparent devotion had made a tremendous impact on him in light of his own disintegrating marriage. But he hardly knew her. They'd only gone out once, had spent barely four hours in each other's company socially. And it hadn't even been a real date.

And yet… Eric couldn't deny that there was at least a kernel of truth in Frank's assessment. He *was* attracted to Kate. To her beauty, certainly, but even more to her person, to who she was, to her essence. Attracted enough to want to get to know her better. And that wasn't good. Because Eric truly believed that in the sight of God he was still married. Through the years he'd never had any trouble remembering that, though countless women had made it clear they were available if he was interested. But he hadn't been. Until now.

Eric reached up with one hand and wearily massaged his temples. He wasn't going to compromise his values by allowing himself to get involved with Kate romantically, even if the lady was willing. Which she wasn't. It was obvious that her late husband had never relinquished his claim on her heart. And even if *he* was free—which he wasn't—getting involved with someone whose heart belonged to another was a recipe for disaster.

Besides, medicine and marriage didn't mix. He'd learned that the hard way. And he'd better not forget it.

Asking Kate to the dinner had probably been a mistake, Eric conceded with a sigh as he pulled the next chart toward him and flipped it open. But he couldn't retract the invitation now. All he could do was make sure it was the last one. Keeping their contact to a minimum was clearly the right thing to do—for everyone's sake.

But if that was true, why did it feel so wrong?

Kate was nervous. She'd spent the entire week second-guessing her decision to go with Eric tonight, less sure with each day that passed about the wisdom of her decision. She'd almost called Amy for another pep talk. But she already knew what her sister would say: "You need to do this, Kate. It's time. It's a first step. Just think of it that way and you'll be fine."

And of course, Amy would be right. After all, it was just a dinner with a nice man who, for whatever reason, had found her engaging enough to want to spend a second evening with her. A man who had no interest in her beyond friendship. So why was she nervous?

"You look pretty, Mommy. Is that a new dress?"

Kate turned back to the mirror. A new dress? Hardly, she thought wryly. The limited money available for new clothes was generally spent on Sarah. Kate had foraged deep in the recesses of her closet for this dress. She'd given away most of her dressier clothes when she sold the house, having neither the room nor the need for them, but she'd kept a couple of things that were classic in style and would be serviceable for any number of functions. This sleeveless linen-like black sheath with a square neckline could be paired with a jacket for a "business" look or worn alone, accented with costume jewelry, for a dressier effect. It had made the "keeper" cut because it was practical. Tonight, a clunky hammered-gold necklace and matching earrings added some glamour to its simple lines, and she'd arranged her hair in a more sophisticated style. The outfit still might not be dressy enough for a black-tie event, Kate acknowledged, but it was the best she could do.

"No, honey. I've had this in my closet for a long time."

"From when Daddy was here?"

The innocent question made Kate's stomach clench, and she gripped the edge of the vanity. She'd bought it shortly after Sarah was born as an incentive to return to her pre-pregnancy measurements, but she'd never worn it.

"Yes, honey. It's as old as you are," she replied, struggling to maintain an even tone.

"Well, I like it. I bet Dr. Eric will, too."

The doorbell rang, and with an, "I'll get it," Sarah scampered off.

Determinedly, Kate put thoughts of the past aside and forced herself to focus on the conversation in the living room as she added a final touch of lipstick.

"Hi, Dr. Eric. Hi, Aunt Anna."

"Hello there, Sarah." Eric's deep voice had a mellow, comforting quality, Kate reflected, her lips curving up slightly.

"Hello, Sarah," Anna greeted the youngster.

On hearing the older woman's voice, Kate felt a pang of guilt. Anna had offered to keep Sarah overnight at her place so Kate and Eric wouldn't have to worry about staying out too late. But Kate had balked. Sarah wasn't even five yet, she had rationalized. It was too soon for her to be gone all night, even though it would have been more convenient for everyone.

"Mommy is almost ready. She looks really pretty. Do you think Mommy is pretty, Dr. Eric?"

There was a momentary pause, and Kate felt hot color surge to her face. But it grew even redder at Eric's husky response. "I think your mommy is beautiful, Sarah."

She had to get out there now, before Sarah asked any other embarrassing questions, Kate thought desperately. Willing the flush on her cheeks to subside, she flipped off the light and hurried down the hall.

"Well, here's Kate now," Anna said brightly. "My dear, you look lovely."

"Thanks, Anna." Her gaze flickered to her escort. "Hello, Eric." She intended to say more, but her voice deserted her as their gazes met. He looked fabulous tonight, she thought in awe. The black tux was a per-

fect complement to his blond hair, and it sat well on his tall, muscular frame, emphasizing his broad shoulders and dignified bearing. Her heart stopped, then raced on. Good heavens, what was she getting herself into? she thought in panic.

Eric took in Kate's attire in one swift, comprehensive glance that missed nothing. Fashionably high heels that accentuated the pleasing line of her legs. A figure-hugging sheath that showed off her slender curves to perfection. A neckline that revealed an expanse of creamy, flawless skin. She looked different tonight, he thought, swallowing with difficulty. Gorgeous. Glamorous. And very desirable. His mouth went dry and his pulse lurched into overdrive.

As his stunned gaze locked with hers, he realized that she seemed equally dazed. Her eyes were slightly glazed and the hand she ran distractedly through her hair was trembling. But no less so than his, he realized, jamming it into his pocket. Electricity fairly sizzled in the air between them.

"Mommy, how come your face is red?" Sarah asked innocently.

Anna stepped in smoothly. "Because she put on extra blush to go with her fancy dress," the older woman replied matter-of-factly. "Now, you two better be on your way or you'll miss dinner."

With an effort Kate dragged her gaze from Eric's. "Yes, y-you're right. I'll just get my purse."

Eric watched her flee down the hall and then drew a shaky breath. He wasn't sure exactly what had happened just now. All he knew was that the smoldering look he'd just exchanged with Kate had left him reeling.

In the sanctuary of her bedroom, Kate forced herself to take several long, slow breaths. What on earth had gone on just now? She felt as if a lightning bolt had zapped her. Eric hadn't even spoken to her, yet they'd connected on some basic level that needed no words. Or had they? Maybe it was all one-sided. Could she have imagined the spark that had flashed between them? It didn't seem possible. And how could she walk back out there and pretend that nothing had happened? But she had no choice. She couldn't acknowledge a thing. The ramifications of doing so were way too scary.

She picked up her purse and walked slowly back down the hall, trying vainly to curb the uncomfortable hammering of her heart. When she stepped back into the living room, her gaze immediately sought Eric's. She searched his eyes, but it was impossible to tell if he'd been as deeply affected by the look that had passed between them as she had been. He seemed as calm and at ease as always. Good. At least one of them was in control.

"Now you two take off," Anna instructed. "And don't hurry. I'm deep into a mystery that will keep me entertained for hours after Sarah goes to bed."

"Ready, Kate?"

Did Eric's voice sound deeper than usual, Kate wondered? Was it slightly uneven? Or was it only her imagination?

"Yes." Her *own* voice was definitely unsteady, she noted with chagrin.

He stepped aside to let her pass, and when he dropped his hand lightly to the small of her back she knew that her last reply was a lie. She wasn't ready at all. Not for tonight. Nor for whatever lay ahead in her relationship with this man.

But then she remembered Amy's comment about the ship. And Amy was right, she told herself resolutely. It was time to chart a new course and set sail.

Chapter Five

As they drove to the downtown hotel where the banquet was being held, Eric could sense Kate's tension. It mirrored his own. To pretend that nothing had happened just now in her apartment would be foolish. To acknowledge it would be dangerous. There was clearly only one way to deal with it: stay away from situations where it might happen again. Frankly, he didn't need the temptation. And she didn't need the stress. His earlier decision to make this their last social excursion was clearly the right one, he told himself resolutely.

However, they still had to get through tonight. He risked a sideways glance at her. She was staring straight ahead, her brow marred by a slight frown, the lines of her body taut with strain. Not good, he concluded. He had been hoping for a repeat of their first outing, when she had relaxed and laughed and had seemed, at least for a little while, less weary and burdened. But tonight they were definitely not off to a good start. This might be their last pseudo "date," but he wanted her to enjoy it. She deserved a pleasant evening. He needed to distract her, introduce a subject that would take her mind off the unexpected chemistry that had erupted between them a few minutes before.

"You know, Mom already seems more like her old self in just the two weeks she's been watching Sarah," he said conversationally.

Kate turned to him. "Does she? I'm glad. It's worked out well for us, too. Sarah looks forward to the time she spends with Anna. What a difference from our brief day-care-center experience!" She sounded a bit breathless, and her tone was a little too bright, but Eric persisted.

"I know there are cases like yours where mothers have to work, but I often think it's a shame that so many of today's kids are being raised by strangers just so the parents can bring in two incomes to support a more extravagant lifestyle. I really think kids would rather have time and attention from their parents than material things."

Kate nodded eagerly, warming to the subject. "You know, that's exactly how Jack and I felt! We waited a long time for Sarah, and we decided that if the Lord ever blessed us with a child, he or she would have at least one full-time parent. That's why I quit my job when she was born. Jack had a good job—he was an engineer—so he was able to provide for us comfortably. Nothing lavish. But then, we didn't need 'lavish.' We just needed each other."

She sighed and turned to stare out the front window, but her eyes were clearly not focused on the road ahead of her. "It was the way I was raised, I guess. We never had a lot when I was growing up," she said softly.

"But we never felt poor, either. Because our home was rich in love. That's what Jack and I wanted for our child. A home filled with love. You know, it's too bad more parents don't realize that kids would rather have your time on a daily basis than a week at some fancy tennis camp in the summer. Sometimes I think parents today spend so much on material things for their children out of guilt—as a way to appease their conscience for the *time* they should have spent instead."

"I couldn't agree more."

Kate looked at him curiously. "I hope you don't think I'm prying, Eric, but... Well, you obviously like kids. And they just as obviously like you. Yet you never had your own."

A flicker of pain crossed his face, but he hid it by turning briefly to glance in the rearview mirror as he debated how to answer Kate's implied question. Hedge or be frank? It was a painful subject, one he'd discussed with only a few trusted, longtime friends. Kate was new in his life. Yet he trusted her. And so he chose to be frank.

"You're right about my feelings with regard to children," he said quietly. "I always assumed that if I ever got married, I'd have my own family. And I guess I also assumed that most people felt that way. Cindy and I somehow never discussed the issue directly. I tried a few times, but as I recall, her answers were always a little vague and noncommittal. I should have pursued it, but I suppose I was afraid of what I'd hear if I pressed the issue. And I didn't want to risk hurting our relationship by upsetting her. I'd figured that once we were married it would just be a natural next step, and any reservations she might have had would evaporate.

"As it turned out, I was wrong. About a lot of things, actually. Cindy didn't want kids, period. They would have 'cramped her style,' as she so succinctly put it. And as much as I wanted children, I didn't want them to have a mother whose heart wasn't in the job. Besides, as she often reminded me, if I was too busy with my career to spend time with her, how would I ever find time to spend with children? And I suppose she had a point," he conceded wearily. "But I still wanted children. Giving up that dream was very difficult."

Kate thought about all the joy Sarah added to her life; how even in her darkest hours, when her heart grieved most deeply for Jack, her daughter had always been the one bright ray of sunlight able to penetrate to the dark, cold corners of her soul and remind her that joy and beauty still lived. But on Eric's darkest days he had struggled alone, not only with disintegration of a marriage but also with the loss of a dream for a family. And now he would always be alone. It was such a waste, she thought, her heart aching for him.

"You would have made a good father, you know," she said gently.

He gave her a crooked grin. "You think so?" His tone was light, but there was a poignant, wistful quality to it that tugged at her heart and made her throat tighten with emotion.

"Yes. As my sister Amy would wisely say, you can tell a lot about a man by the way he treats children. And you can tell a lot about a man by the way children treat *him*. According to her, children have almost a sixth sense about people. Using Sarah—who's generally very shy around strangers—as a yardstick, you stand pretty tall. So, yes, I think you would have made a great dad.''

Eric felt his neck redden at the compliment. Very few things made him uncomfortable, but praise was at the top of the list. So he quickly refocused the attention on Kate. "I can hear the affection in your voice when you mention your sister. I take it you and she are close?''

"Yes. It's too bad she lives in Tennessee. We have to be content with weekly phone calls," she told him with a sigh.

"Tennessee isn't too far. Don't you visit occasionally?''

"Not as often as we'd like. Her husband, Cal, is an attorney *and* a part-time ranger in Great Smoky Mountains National Park, so his busy season is summer. They can never get away then, and I'm teaching the rest of the year. Besides, it's tough traveling with three small children—four-year-old twins and a six-month-old.''

He gave a low whistle. "She *does* have her hands full.''

Kate smiled. "That's putting it mildly. She also hosts a bi-weekly program on a Christian cable station in Knoxville. Anyway, Sarah, Mom and I always went down in the spring, and then again at Thanksgiving. But that's about it.''

"Thanksgiving in the Smokies sounds nice," he remarked with a smile.

"It is. Especially at Amy's. She's become quite the earth mother. They live in a log cabin, and she makes quilts and bakes homemade bread and cans vegetables. It's an amazing transition, considering that in her twenties she was an absolutely gung-ho career woman who liked bright lights and traveling in the fast lane and thought life simply ceased to exist outside the city limits.''

''What happened?''

''Cal.''

''Ah. True love.''

''Uh-huh. It wasn't that she changed for him. She just discovered that all that time she'd been living a lie. Somewhere along the way she'd bought into the notion that success is only measured in dollars and prestige and power. But she was never happy, even though she had all those things. It took Cal to make her realize that.''

''That's quite a story, Kate. Sort of reaffirms your belief in happy endings.''

She smiled softly. ''Yeah, it does. They're a great couple.'' As Eric turned into the curving drive of the hotel, Kate sent him a startled look. ''You mean we're here already?''

''See how times flies when you're having fun?'' She smiled, and he was gratified to note that she now seemed much more relaxed. ''Shall we go in and be wined and dined?''

''I think that's what we're here for,'' she replied.

Eric didn't have Kate to himself again until after dessert. As a board member, he knew many of the guests and it seemed that all of them wanted to spend a few minutes talking with him during the cocktail hour. Throughout the meal Kate was kept occupied by an elderly man seated to her right. Only when their dinner companions rose to mingle with other guests did Eric have a few minutes alone with her.

"You seem to have made a friend in Henri," he remarked, nodding toward the older man who was now greeting some guests at a nearby table.

Kate followed Eric's glance and smiled. "He's a fascinating person. You'd never guess by looking at him that he was an underground fighter with the French Resistance in World War II, would you?"

Eric stared at Kate. He'd known Henri Montand, a major contributor to this event, for ten years. But it seemed that Kate had learned more about his background over one dinner than he had in a decade.

"You're kidding!"

"No. You didn't know?"

He shook his head ruefully. "Speaking of having a way with people... I may be pretty good with kids, but you obviously have a knack with adults." Kate flushed at his compliment, and he found that quality in her endearing—and utterly appealing. "So, are you having fun?" he asked, trying unsuccessfully to minimize the sudden huskiness in his voice. Fortunately, Kate didn't seem to notice.

"Oh, yes! This is a lovely event." She glanced around appreciatively at the fresh flower arrangements on the tables, the crystal chandeliers and the orchestra just beginning to tune up.

"The fund-raising committee generally does a nice job. But most importantly, the organization does good work. Abused kids need all the help they can get."

"You really take your commitment to children seriously, don't you? On and off the job."

"It's pretty hard to leave it at the office," he admitted. "But I do too much sometimes, I guess. That's what Cindy always said, anyway. And since the divorce, I've gotten even more involved. Frank's always saying that I'm a driven man. Even Mom's been telling me to get a life. And they're right. My terms on two boards are up at the end of the year and I've already decided not to renew them. But I'll stay involved with this one. I've been on the board for almost ten years and—''

"Eric! Kate!"

They glanced up, and Kate recognized the man bustling toward them as an energetic, fortyish board member Eric had introduced her to earlier. "Listen, help us out, will you? We need some people to kick off the dancing. I think if I get five or six of the board members out on the floor, everyone will loosen up. Thanks, guys." Without giving them a chance to respond, he hurried off.

Kate stared after him, then glanced at Eric uncertainly. "I haven't danced in years."

"Neither have I."

She gave a nervous laugh. "Honestly, Eric, I don't even think I remember how. That was about the only thing Jack couldn't do. I haven't danced since my wedding."

"I haven't danced in six or seven years."

"So should we just pass? I mean, I'd like to help out, but..." She lifted her shoulders helplessly.

Eric looked at her thoughtfully. It would be easy to agree. And probably wise. But as he gazed at Kate, bathed in golden light from the centerpiece candle, the creamy skin of her neck and collarbone glowing warmly, the delicate curve of her neck illuminated by the flickering flame, he was suddenly overcome by a compelling need to hold her in his arms and sway to romantic music. It would be a memory of their brief time together that he could dust off when the nights got long and he was in a melancholy mood, or on those rare occasions when he let himself indulge in fantasy and wonder how differently his life might have turned out if he'd met someone like Kate a dozen years ago.

"I'm willing to give it a try if you are."

Her eyes grew wide. "Are you serious?"

"Absolutely."

"But I'm really not very good, Eric. I'll probably step all over your feet."

"I'm more worried about stepping on yours. Come on, we'll muddle through." He stood and held out his hand.

Kate hesitated. It was true that her dancing skills were extremely rusty. And it was also true that she was worried about looking awkward and embarrassing Eric. But she was even more worried about the close proximity that dancing entailed. It was one thing to sit next to this virile man in the car or at the table, and quite another to be held in his arms. She wasn't exactly sure how she would handle the closeness. But there seemed to be no way to gracefully decline. So she took a deep breath and placed her hand in his.

"You may be sorry," she warned, her voice not quite steady.

"I don't think so."

As he led her out to the dance floor, the orchestra began playing "Unforgettable." He glanced down at her and grinned. "You know, if we're both as bad as we claim, that's exactly what this dance might be."

Her insides were quaking, but she managed to smile. "You could be right."

As it turned out, the dance really was unforgettable. In every way.

From the moment he drew her into his arms, she felt as if she'd come home. They danced together perfectly, moving effortlessly to the beat of the music. And once she realized she didn't have to worry about her feet, she was able to focus on other things—the spicy scent of his after-shave, the way he tenderly folded her right hand in his left, tucking it protectively against his solid chest, and the strong, sure feel of his other hand splayed across her back, guiding her firmly but gently.

Kate closed her eyes and let his touch and the romantic music work their magic. It had been a long time, such a very long time, since she'd been held this way; since she'd felt so safe and protected and—the word *cherished* came to mind. Which was strange. After all, she barely knew Eric. But something about the way he held her made her feel all of those things. Of course, it might just be her imagination. But, real or not, she intended to enjoy the moment, because it might never come again. With a contented sigh, she relaxed against him.

Eric felt Kate's sudden relaxation, and instinctively he drew her closer, tilting his head slightly so that her lustrous hair brushed his cheek. Then he closed his eyes and inhaled, savoring the faint, pleasing floral fragrance that emanated from her skin. She felt good in his arms, he reflected; soft and feminine and very, very appealing. He swallowed with difficulty. *Dear Lord, why did you send someone like this my way?* he cried silently, overcome by a sudden sense of anguish and regret. *I made a vow in Your sight on my wedding day that I don't want to break. But I'm lonely, Lord. And*

*Kate is getting harder and harder to resist. Her sweet-
ness and values and kind heart are like a ray of sun
in my life. I'm drawn to her, Lord. Powerfully. Please
help me find the strength to do what is right.*

By the time the music ended, Kate was fairly quivering. And Eric didn't look much steadier, she reflected, as—with obvious reluctance—he released her.
The hand that rested at the small of her back as he
guided her toward their table felt about as unsteady as
her legs.

"Eric! I knew you were here somewhere but I just
couldn't seem to find you in this crowd."

They turned in unison as a man in his mid-fifties
with salt-and-pepper hair approached them.

"Hello, Reverend Jacobs." Eric's voice sounded
husky, she noted. But at least it was working. She
wasn't sure about her own. "It's quite a turnout, isn't
it?"

"It gets bigger every year, which is very gratifying."

"Reverend, I'd like you to meet Kate Nolan. Kate,
Reverend Carl Jacobs, my minister."

"Nice to meet you, Mrs. Nolan." The man extended
his hand, and Kate found her fingers engulfed in a firm,
somehow reassuring clasp. She stared at the minister,
struck by the kindness and serenity in his eyes. He
radiated calm, like someone who was at peace with life,
who understood the vagaries of this world and had not
only accepted them, but had found a way to move beyond them. He seemed, somehow, like a man with answers. The kind of answers Kate had been searching
for.

Their gazes held for a long moment, until at last Kate

found her voice. "It's nice to meet you, too. Eric has spoken very highly of you."

"And also of you. I've met your daughter. She's charming."

"Thank you."

Suddenly Eric reached inside his jacket and retrieved his pager. He scanned the message, then frowned. "Would you two excuse me while I make a quick phone call?"

"Of course," Kate replied.

"I'll keep Mrs. Nolan company," the reverend promised.

They watched as Eric threaded his way through the crowd, then disappeared.

"He works too hard," Reverend Jacobs remarked. "But it's difficult to fault such dedication. And he's a fine doctor."

"I agree."

"Eric has mentioned you, Mrs. Nolan. Have you known each other long?"

"Please call me Kate. Actually, Eric and I have a somewhat unusual history. We met—if you could call it that—five years ago, when my husband was seriously injured in a car accident. Eric saved his life."

The minister's eyebrows rose. "Is that right? Eric never mentioned it. But then, I'm not surprised. To use an old cliché, he isn't one to blow his own horn. But I understood from Eric that you were a widow."

"Yes. My husband lived for several months after the accident, but he never regained consciousness."

"I'm so sorry, Kate. It must have been a very difficult time for you. Sarah would have been just a baby, I'm sure."

She swallowed and nodded. "She was six weeks old. She needed me, and so I managed to get through the days. But it was almost like my own life ended in some ways when Jack died," she said quietly.

"I know what you mean. I lost my wife of thirty years to cancer just five months ago. She left a void that can never be filled."

Kate's face softened in sympathy. "I'm so sorry, Reverend."

"Thank you. It's been a difficult time. But the Lord has sustained me."

A flash of pain and bitterness swept through her. "I wish I could say the same. I always felt He'd deserted me."

"Many people feel that way in the face of tragedy," Reverend Jacobs returned in an understanding tone that held no censure. "But often the opposite actually happens. We think the Lord hasn't answered our prayers, so we turn away. But you know, He always does answer us. It's just that sometimes it's not the answer we want to hear."

Kate frowned. "I've never thought of it quite that way before. But why would He take someone like Jack, who was so young and had so much to offer? Why would He not only take my husband, but deprive Sarah of a father? What sense does that make?"

"The Lord's ways are often difficult to understand, Kate. And I certainly don't have all the answers," the minister said gently. "But maybe together we could find a few. I'd certainly be happy to talk things through with you. Why don't you stop by some day?"

Kate thought about Eric's comment at the barbecue—that Reverend Jacobs had helped him through some difficult times. Might he be able to do the same for her? Help her find the sense of peace that he so obviously had, even in the face of a recent, tragic loss? It seemed like an option that might bear exploring.

"I just might do that, Reverend."

"Please do." He extracted a card from his pocket and handed it to her, then glanced over her shoulder. "Well, here comes your host." He waved at Eric, who was weaving through the crowd, then turned to Kate and extended his hand. "I have several more people to see before I leave tonight. It was a pleasure to meet you. And do think about stopping by."

"I will."

Eric rejoined her a moment later, and the concern on his face made her breath catch in her throat. "What's wrong? Is Sarah..."

"Sarah's fine," he reassured her quickly, noting her sudden pallor. "That was my exchange. I'm on call tonight. One of my patients has been in an accident, and her parents are on their way to the hospital with her now. I promised to meet them. Normally I'd just let the emergency room handle it, but she's got asthma as well and I thought a familiar face might help calm her down. She's only eight."

"Of course." She reached for her purse and tucked the minister's card inside.

"Kate, I'm sorry about this," Eric said regretfully. "I wanted us to have a nice evening."

"But we have! The dinner was lovely, and we even got to dance. That's more than I've done in a long time. Please don't worry about it."

He gazed down into Kate's sincere eyes and felt a lump form in his throat. He remembered Cindy's atti-

tude on occasions when they'd had to cut a social evening short—resentful, put-upon, angry. It had put a
strain on their relationship for days. Of course, Cindy
had been through it many times. This was a first for
Kate. Maybe, in time, she'd grow to feel the same way.
But somehow he didn't think so. Not that the theory
would ever be put to the test, he reminded himself
firmly.

"Thanks for understanding," he said quietly.

She shrugged off his gratitude. "Don't be silly. If I
was a parent with an injured child, I'd want *my* doctor
there. It's the right thing to do."

"Nevertheless, I appreciate it. I'd take you home
first, but the hospital is so close. How about if I call
you a cab?"

"Why don't I just go with you?"

That was an offer he'd never heard before. "To the
hospital?" he asked in surprise.

"Would that be okay?"

"Sure. I'd appreciate the company," he said honestly. "But it could be a while," he warned.

"If you're delayed I can just get a cab from there. I
don't mind waiting, Eric." Which was true. She really
didn't want their evening to end just yet.

"Okay, if you're sure."

As they turned to go, she expected him to place his
hand at the small of her back and guide her toward the
door, as had become his custom. But instead, he surprised her by taking her hand in his, linking their fingers and squeezing gently. The smile he gave her was
warm and somehow intimate.

"Thanks for being a good sport."

As he led her out of the ballroom, Kate savored the

feel of his strong fingers entwined with hers. And she wondered about Cindy's customary reaction to an interruption such as this. Not good, apparently, considering how grateful—and taken aback—Eric had been by her acceptance of it. She was beginning to form a picture of his married life. And it wasn't pretty.

A movement on the other side of the waiting room caught her eye, and Kate looked up from her magazine. The young couple whose daughter had been injured had risen anxiously, privy to something in the corridor hidden from Kate's view. A moment later Eric entered and walked toward them. Though they spoke in low tones, their voices carried clearly.

"How is she, Doctor?" The man's face was lined with anxiety, and Kate could tell even from across the room that his wife had a death grip on his hand. Her heart contracted in sympathy, and she blinked back sudden tears. She knew what it was like to wait in a cold, sterile anteroom for news about someone you loved.

"She'll be fine, Mr. Thomas. Let's sit down for a minute. Mrs. Thomas?" Eric nodded toward a cluster of chairs and gently guided the mother toward one, clearly attuned to the woman's emotional distress. Kate was impressed by his astuteness—and his thoughtfulness. In a medical world that was often clinical and impersonal, Eric appeared to be an admirable exception. Which somehow didn't surprise her.

When they were seated, he spoke again, his tone calm and reassuring. "Emily has lots of scrapes and bruises, but nothing requiring stitches. Her arm is broken—in two places, actually—but they're clean breaks and should heal just fine. Dr. West is a fine orthopedic surgeon and he took care of everything. She was having a little trouble with her breathing when I first arrived, but we got that under control very quickly. Once I started talking to her about your vacation to Walt Disney World, she calmed down and the asthma wasn't a problem. We'd like to keep her overnight just to make sure she's not in too much pain and monitor her breathing. There should be no problem with her going home in the morning."

The relief on the young couple's faces was visible from across the room, Kate noted discreetly.

"I can't thank you enough for coming in tonight, Doctor," the woman said gratefully, her voice thick with tears. "We told her all the way here in the car that you were coming, and that helped to keep her calm. We were so afraid she'd have an attack!"

"No thanks are necessary, Mrs. Thomas. I'm just doing my job."

"You do a lot more than that," the girl's father corrected him. "Most doctors just send you to the emergency room. They don't show up themselves. This means a lot to us. Especially when it's obvious we interrupted a special event." He nodded toward Eric's tux.

"I was glad to do it. I'll stop by in the morning and check on Emily, and by lunchtime she'll be ready to go home. Just tell her not to play soccer quite so aggressively in the future," he said with a grin.

"Do you think maybe we should take her off the team?" the man asked anxiously.

"Not at all. We've got her asthma under control. And kids need to run and play and stretch their wings.

Reasonable caution is prudent. Excessive caution is stifling. Sometimes accidents happen, but that's part of living.'' Eric rose. ''They're getting ready to move her to a room, so let me take you down to her and you can walk with her.''

Eric glanced at Kate and smiled as he ushered the couple out, mouthing, ''I'll be right back.'' She nodded.

When he reappeared a few minutes later, she was waiting at the doorway. He smiled at her ruefully. ''You look ready to leave.''

''Let's just say hospitals aren't my favorite places,'' she replied lightly, but he heard the pain in her voice. His gut clenched at the echo of sadness in her eyes and he frowned.

''I'm sorry, Kate. I didn't even think about that. I shouldn't have let you come. Instead of leaving you with pleasant memories of tonight, I've dredged up unhappy ones.''

''I wanted to come,'' she insisted. ''And I'm glad I did. It wasn't as hard as I thought it might be.''

He took her arm and guided her purposefully toward the door. ''But there's no reason to hang around now. It's my second trip today, anyway.'' He glanced at his watch and his frown deepened. ''It's probably too late to go back to the dance. Would you like to stop and get a cup of coffee on the way home?''

She looked up at him. He'd mentioned he was on call this weekend. And that he'd already made one trip to the hospital today. There were fine lines at the corners of his eyes, and slight shadows beneath them. Much as she'd like to extend the evening, she shook her head. ''It's been a long week, Eric. And there's no reason to keep your mother up any later than necessary. Let's head back."

He studied her for a moment. "Are you sure?"

"Of course. But I had a good time tonight, despite the interruption."

He chuckled. "I guess we should look on the bright side," he said as they reached his car and he opened the door for her.

She glanced at him curiously. "What do you mean?"

"Well, we may have ended up at a hospital, but at least it wasn't because of any broken toes."

She smiled. He had a good sense of humor. And he wasn't afraid to laugh at himself. She liked that. "Good point. Actually, I think we did quite well for two very out-of-practice dancers."

Eric almost suggested that they polish up their skills another night, but he caught himself in time. There wouldn't be another time, he reminded himself soberly. It was too dangerous, because Kate was easy to be with, and he knew with absolute certainty that she could very easily become a part of his life—an important part. But given his situation, all he could offer her was friendship.

And his feelings were already running way too deep for that.

Chapter Six

Kate drew a deep breath, then reached up and rang the bell on the parsonage. She wasn't sure exactly why she had followed through and made an appointment with Reverend Jacobs, except that she had been struck by the calm and peace he radiated even in the face of personal tragedy. She sensed that he had found the answers to some of life's harder questions, and that he might also have some of the answers *she* needed. It couldn't hurt to find out, especially since Anna had agreed to keep Sarah for an extra hour after school so Kate could take care of some "personal" business.

The door swung open, and Reverend Jacobs smiled at her kindly. "Kate. It's good to see you again. Come in."

She stepped into the foyer, and as the minister led her toward his office he paused beside an older woman seated at a word processor.

"Kate, this is Margaret Stephens. She's been with me for...how long, Margaret?"

The woman smiled indulgently. "Twenty-two years, Reverend."

"That's right, twenty-two years. She keeps my professional life in order. I'd be lost without her. Margaret, Kate Nolan."

They exchanged greetings, then the minister ushered his visitor into the office and closed the door. "I know you're on a tight schedule, Kate. Please make yourself comfortable." He indicated a small sitting area off to one side. "Can I offer you some coffee?"

"No, thanks. I've had my one cup for the day. My husband was the real coffee drinker in the family," she said, her lips curving up in affectionate remembrance.

Reverend Jacobs filled a mug and sat in a chair at right angles to hers. "Would you mind telling me a little bit about him, Kate? I can see that he's still a very important part of your life. I have a feeling that to know you, I also need to know him."

"I—I hardly know where to begin, Reverend," she faltered, her smile fading.

"How about telling me how you met?"

Under his gentle questioning, Kate found herself recounting their first meeting, courtship and eventual engagement. Halting phrases eventually gave way to a flood of words as she spoke about their wedding, their early years as a married couple, and their joy at Sarah's birth. Only when she came to the accident, the subsequent seven-month nightmare and her feelings of confusion and abandonment, did she once more struggle to find words.

"At first I refused to accept the prognosis," she said, her voice subdued and laced with pain. "I just couldn't believe the Lord would allow Jack to be paralyzed or to…to die. I prayed constantly, not only for my sake, but for Sarah's. I didn't want her to grow up without a father. I had faith, and every time I went to the hospital I believed there would be a breakthrough. But the months went by with no change, and eventually Jack was moved to a long-term-care facility. That's when I began to lose hope. Seven months after the accident, he died.''

"Tell me about how you felt then, Kate," Reverend Jacobs said gently.

She lifted her shoulders wearily. "Numb. Devastated. Angry. Guilty. Confused. A whole tangle of emotions. I still feel a lot of them."

"Can you talk to me about the anger and guilt?"

She drew a deep breath. "I was angry at God," she said slowly. "I still am. And I was angry at Jack—which was totally illogical and only made me feel guilty. The accident wasn't his fault. But I still felt as if he'd deserted me. And then I kept thinking, if only he'd worn his seat belt. I should have reminded him to buckle up. I usually did. But it just didn't occur to me that night. So that added to the guilt."

"None of those feelings are abnormal, Kate. I experienced many of them myself when my wife died. I felt guilty, too, thinking that if only I'd insisted she go to the doctor sooner, she might have lived. And when she died, I was angry. She was taken from me just when we were reaching the stage in our lives when we'd planned to travel and spend more time together. All of the thoughts and emotions you mentioned are part of the natural grieving process. Knowing that others have gone through the same things often helps. Have you shared your feelings with anyone?"

"No. I just...couldn't find the words. And then I kept trying to figure out why God would take Jack from us. It just didn't make sense. I began to think that maybe...maybe I was being punished for something I did wrong," she said in a small voice.

The minister nodded sympathetically. "People often feel as you did when they lose someone they love—that it's their own fault in some way. But that's not the case, Kate. Jack's death had nothing to do with you. It was simply his time to go to the Lord. We can spend our lives asking why about such things, but that's an exercise in futility. The better path is to simply let go and admit that even though we can't understand the Lord's ways, we accept them. That's the only way to find peace in this world. But it's not always easy."

She nodded, and hot tears welled in her eyes. "I know. I've been trying to find that peace for a long time."

"You took a good first step today."

Kate shook her head sadly. "I'm not sure about that, Reverend. To be frank, I only came because I'm desperate. You found peace because your faith is strong. Mine isn't, or it would have sustained me through this trial. Instead, it died with Jack. So I guess on top of everything else, I've failed God." Her voice broke on the last word.

Reverend Jacobs leaned forward intently. "Let me tell you something, Kate. Doubts and despair don't make you a bad person. They just mean you're human. That's how the Lord created us, with all the weaknesses and frailties that entails. He doesn't expect perfection. He knows we stumble and lose our way. In fact, the history of Christianity is filled with holy men and women who experienced a dark night of the soul at some point in their lives. The Lord didn't disown them because of that, even when they disowned Him. He just patiently waited for them to come home. That's the beauty of our faith, Kate. The Lord is always ready to welcome us back, no matter how far we wander, once we open our hearts to Him.''

Kate saw nothing but sincerity and compassion in the minister's eyes, and a little flicker of hope leaped to life in her soul. "I'd like to believe that, Reverend. I'd like to try to find my way back. But I—I don't know how."

"As I said, you've already taken the first step by coming here today. And I'll do all I can to help you. May I also suggest that you join your lovely little girl at Sunday services? Just hearing the words of Scripture may offer you some comfort and guidance. You probably won't find what you're seeking in one or two visits, but if you persist, in God's time you will."

Kate wasn't convinced. But clearly Reverend Jacobs was. And her faith *had* been important to her at one time. Perhaps, with the minister's help, it could be again.

Kate nervously adjusted the belt on her navy blue knit dress, then ran a brush through her hair. She knew Eric would be surprised when he discovered he had two guests for services today. She probably should have called and warned him. But she hadn't decided for sure about going until this morning. And besides, he *had* told her she was welcome anytime. She hoped that was still true, considering she hadn't heard from him since the night of the dinner dance, a week before.

But then, why should she? Their outings had been defined as "favors," not dates. He probably didn't need any more of those. Neither of them was in the market for romance, but she had hoped that maybe they could be friends.

The doorbell interrupted her thoughts, and she headed toward the living room. "I'll get it," she told Sarah as she passed the bathroom. "You finish up those teeth."

When she reached the door, she took a deep breath to steady her suddenly rapid pulse, then smiled before she pulled it open. "Good morning, Eric."

His own smile of welcome turned into a look of inquiry as his gaze swept over her. "You're awfully dressed up for grading papers."

She flushed. "Actually, I thought I might— That is, if the invitation is still open I'd like to join you for church today."

For a brief moment before he shuttered his emotions she thought she saw a flash of apprehension—and dismay—in his eyes, and her stomach clenched painfully. She stepped aside to let him enter, then turned to face him nervously.

"I stopped by to see Reverend Jacobs Friday after school, and we had a long talk. You were right. He's a good listener. I felt better about…about a lot of things after we spoke. He suggested I try coming back to church, so I decided to join you today, if that's okay."

"Mom will be delighted."

A telling response, she reflected, suddenly acutely embarrassed. His *mother* would be delighted. Not him. She hadn't imagined his reluctance. For some reason he was pulling back, retreating from the relationship he'd initiated with her, she realized as a flush rose to her cheeks.

"Listen, Eric, maybe this isn't such a good idea. After all, I have my own car. It isn't as if we have to go together. I don't want to impose and take you out of your way when there's no need. I should have called you earlier and just said we'd see you there. I'm sorry to—"

The words died in her throat as he reached over and touched her arm.

"Kate."

She stared at him with wide, uncertain eyes. He looked down at her, frowning. She'd obviously picked up on his sudden discomfort, he realized. His resolve to stay away from her was shaky at best, but he'd figured it would hold if he just stopped by once a week to pick up Sarah and only saw Kate long enough to say hello. Her unexpected decision to go to church complicated things tremendously. But that was *his* problem. He *had* invited her to join them. She didn't strike him as the kind of woman who reached out easily, and his response had been far from enthusiastic. He needed to reassure her without telling her the real reason for his hesitation.

"You surprised me, that's all. I think it's great you've decided to go back to church."

She looked into his eyes, searching for the consternation she'd seen earlier, but it was gone. Had she imagined it? she wondered in confusion.

"We can go on our own in the future," she offered, her voice still uncertain. "I just thought it might be easier this first time to be with people we know."

His hand still rested on her arm, and its warmth

seeped through the thin fabric of her dress as he gave her a gentle squeeze. "We'll talk about the future later, okay? Let's just worry about today for now."

It was a vague answer, but his voice was kind and his smile genuine. Besides, the future might not even be an issue. She might never go back to church again. She wasn't convinced that it would make that much difference, despite Reverend Jacobs's confidence.

But half an hour later, sitting in a pew beside Eric, she had the oddest sense of homecoming. As she listened to the words of Scripture, joined in the old familiar hymns and reflected on the sermon appropriately titled "All You Must Do Is Knock," she was surprised at just how much the experience touched her heart. And Reverend Jacobs's warm greeting afterward made her feel good—and welcome.

"I'm so glad you came, Kate," he said, taking her hand in a firm grip.

"So am I."

"Eric, Anna, good to see you both. Hello, Sarah."

"Hello," the little girl said shyly, staying close beside Kate.

"You know, I bet you'd enjoy our Sunday school," he told the youngster before turning back to Kate. "The fall session is just starting. Sarah would be most welcome."

"Thank you. I'll think about it."

"Just give us a call if you'd like to enroll her."

They moved on then, so others could speak with the minister, and she reached for Sarah's hand as Eric cupped her elbow.

"You'll join us for breakfast, won't you?"

"Can we, Mommy?" Sarah asked eagerly.

Kate glanced quickly at Eric, but his face was unreadable.

"Of course you can," Anna chimed in. "We won't take no for an answer, will we, Eric?"

"Absolutely not," he replied firmly.

"I really don't want to intrude on your time together," Kate protested.

"It's three-to-one, Kate," Eric said with a smile that made her feel warm all over. "Give it up."

She swallowed. "Okay, you win. For today, anyway."

"Oh, goody!" Sarah exclaimed, hopping from one foot to the other. "Can I have pancakes?" she asked Eric.

"Of course."

"This is the best Sunday I can ever remember," she declared happily.

Kate didn't respond. It was one of her best Sundays in a long time, too. But she had an uncomfortable feeling that it wasn't one of Eric's. And for some reason that made her spirits, which had been buoyed by the church service, take a sudden nosedive.

"Did you and Kate have some sort of misunderstanding?"

Eric frowned and positioned the phone more comfortably against his ear as he closed the chart in front of him. "Hello, Mom," he replied wryly.

"Oh. Hello. Well, did you?"

"Did I what?"

"Have a misunderstanding with Kate," she repeated impatiently.

"No."

"Then why won't she go to church with us this Sunday?"

Eric's frown deepened. "You mean she isn't?"

"No. She stayed for a cup of tea today when she picked up Sarah and told me that they would be going by themselves from now on, and to please let you know and thank you for all your help."

Kate had obviously picked up on his momentary panic last Sunday when she'd announced that she was going to accompany them. But maybe that was for the best, he reasoned. He didn't want to hurt her, but he couldn't afford to get too close, because if he did, they could *both* be hurt. Badly. Given his marital status and the demands of his profession—which had ruined one marriage already—she was a temptation he didn't need.

"Eric? Are you still there?" his mother prompted.

"Yes."

"So did something happen between you two to upset her?"

"I haven't even talked to her all week, Mom."

"Why not?"

"I hardly know her."

"Well, I'd hoped you'd be trying to remedy that. Women like Kate don't come along very often, you know. She's a wonderful person."

"She's also still in love with her husband."

"Of course she is. I'm sure she always will be. Love like that doesn't die, Eric." His mother's voice suddenly grew subdued and sad, and his heart contracted in sympathy—and in shared loss. His father's death had been extremely hard on both of them, leaving a gap that could never be filled. "But that doesn't mean you can't ever love anyone else. And I just thought…'' Her voice trailed off.

Eric sighed. He knew what she thought—that he needed to find someone new. But aside from the fact that he still considered himself married, there were other pitfalls to a relationship: namely, the demands of his profession.

"That's not an option, Mom," he said gently but firmly.

"But Eric, you've been divorced for almost five years," she argued. "Cindy is remarried. It doesn't seem right for you to be alone. You should have a wife and family."

"I tried that once. It didn't work."

There was a brief hesitation before she quietly declared, "Maybe it was just the wrong woman."

Eric's eyebrows rose in surprise. Though his mother was usually outspoken in her opinion, she'd never before come this close to saying what he'd always suspected she felt about his marriage: that he and Cindy had not been a good match.

"Maybe," he admitted. "But it's too late now for second-guessing."

Her sigh came clearly over the wire. "Sometimes I think you're too hard on yourself, Eric. I'm sure the Lord doesn't expect you to spend the rest of your life alone when the divorce wasn't even your fault. As I recall, Cindy was the one who wanted out. You were willing to work at it."

"I'm not blameless, Mom. I have a demanding career, and it got in the way of our relationship. Marriage and medicine just don't seem to mix."

"That's nonsense," she declared briskly. "Most

doctors are married and they manage just fine. Look at Frank.''

"Well, maybe he knows some secret I don't.''

"There's no secret, Eric. It just takes love and understanding on both sides.''

"I can't debate that with you, Mom. All I know is that it didn't work for me. And even if I was free, I'm not willing to take that risk again. Besides, Kate obviously isn't interested. So let it rest. It's probably for the best.''

Eric knew his mother wasn't happy with his response. She wanted him to have another chance at love. And as he hung up the receiver, he had to admit that he wanted that, too. Especially now. The hours he'd spent in Kate's company had given him a glimpse of the life he might have had with the right woman. But his error in judgment had cost him dearly, he thought with a disheartened sigh. And he was still paying the price.

Kate read the thermometer gauge worriedly. One hundred and two.

"I don't feel good, Mommy,'' Sarah whimpered.

Kate smoothed the hair from her daughter's damp forehead with a slightly unsteady hand. "I know, honey. I'm going to call Dr. Eric right now. You just lie here and be very quiet, okay?''

Kate tucked the blankets around Sarah, then headed for the phone to call Eric's exchange. She also spoke with Anna to let her know she was keeping Sarah home tomorrow.

"It's probably just a flu bug, Kate,'' the older woman reassured her. "Don't worry too much. Children get these things, you know. They bounce back quickly. When did she get sick?"

"A couple of hours ago, right before dinner. It just came on suddenly. She was fine this morning and had a great time at Sunday school."

"Oh, you must have gone to the later service, then. Eric was concerned when we didn't see you at church."

Was he? Kate wondered with a wistfulness that surprised—and disconcerted—her as she rang off. Deep inside she'd like to think his concern was prompted by more than polite consideration. After all, they'd spent two very enjoyable social evenings together. And she liked him. A lot. Too much, maybe, because the feelings he awakened in her made her feel disloyal to Jack. And she wasn't sure how to deal with that. But since he seemed to be putting a distance between them, it apparently wasn't something she needed to worry about, she reminded herself firmly.

But he wasn't putting distance between them today, Kate realized when she opened the door forty-five minutes later and found Eric. Her eyes widened as she noted the well-worn jeans that clung to his long, lean legs and the blue cotton shirt with rolled-up sleeves, open at the neck. Kate had never seen him dressed so informally before, and the effect was...well, stunning. In this rugged clothing, he literally took her breath away. She clung to the edge of the door and stared at him.

"Kate? Are you okay?"

Okay? No, she wasn't okay. In fact, her hand on the edge of the door was trembling. Which was ridiculous! She tried to get a grip. She barely knew this man, she reminded herself. They were practically strangers. Yes, he was handsome. Yes, he was nice. Yes, she found herself attracted to him at some basic level that she didn't understand. But he wasn't in the market for romance, and neither was she. She needed to remember that. She drew a shaky breath and somehow found her voice.

"Yes. I'm fine. But Sarah's not."

"That's why I'm here."

He held up his black bag, which had somehow escaped Kate's notice. Her gaze had gotten stuck on his broad shoulders and muscular chest. "A house call?" she said in surprise, her voice slightly breathless.

He smiled and shrugged. "Mom said you sounded really worried."

Kate stepped aside and motioned him in. "I am. But I didn't expect you to come over. It's your day off, isn't it? The answering service said Frank was taking the calls this weekend."

"He is. But I told him I'd handle this one."

"Why? I mean, you don't do this for all your patients, do you?"

He gazed down at her, and the blue of his eyes seemed to intensify. "No, Kate, I don't."

She stared at him, and her mouth suddenly went dry. He'd answered her second question, but not her first. Which was probably just as well, because she wasn't ready to deal with the answer she might get. At least, not yet. Nervously she tucked her hair behind her ear and looked away. "Well, I—I appreciate it, Eric. Sarah's back here."

Eric followed as she led the way down the short hallway. He was glad she hadn't pressed for an answer to her first question, because he wasn't sure himself why he had come. There had been no need to make a house call. Frank could easily have dealt with the situation by phone. But he'd experienced such a letdown when he didn't see Kate in church this morning that he'd grasped at the first excuse to see her. It wasn't wise, of course. But when it came to her, his heart seemed more in control of his actions than his mind was. Which was a problem he needed to address—and soon.

"Dr. Eric came to see you, honey."

Eric smiled at Sarah as he followed Kate into the charmingly decorated little girl's room and sat down on the bed beside his patient. "Hello, Sarah. I heard you were sick."

"Uh-huh. I threw up."

He glanced at Kate.

She nodded. "Twice in the last hour. And her temperature is still a hundred and two."

"Well, that doesn't sound like much fun." He snapped his bag open as he spoke. "I'd better take a look. Is that all right with you, Sarah?"

"I guess so. You aren't going to give me a shot, are you?"

He chuckled. "Not today. I'm just going to listen to your heart and look in your ears and check out those tonsils."

He conversed easily with Sarah while he did a quick exam. When he finished he removed the stethoscope from around his neck and placed it back in his bag.

"Well, little lady, I think you have the flu. But you know what? You should feel a whole lot better by tomorrow. In the meantime, I want you to drink a lot of soda and water and juice and take aspirin whenever your mom gives them to you. Okay?''

"Okay."

He turned to Kate. "Do you have any white soda?"

She nodded. "I'll get some—and the aspirin."

As Kate disappeared down the hall, he turned back to find Sarah studying him quite seriously. "Dr. Eric, do you have a little girl of your own?" she asked suddenly.

A pang of regret ricocheted through him, almost painful in its intensity, but he managed to smile. "No."

"Do you wish you had a little girl?"

"Sometimes."

"Sometimes I wish I had a daddy, too." She pointed to a picture of Jack on her bedside table. "He was my daddy. Mommy says he watches out for me from heaven now, but I wish I had a daddy who could hold me in his lap and tell me stories."

"I wish you did, too, Sarah." Eric reached over and smoothed the hair back from her flushed face as his throat constricted. If everything had gone the way he'd planned, he would have his own children right now, and a wife who loved him. But he'd never have the former. Nor had he ever had the latter, he thought sadly. Through the years he had gradually come to realize that Cindy had never really loved him—not in the fullest sense of that word. It had been a hard thing to accept. It still was.

"Maybe you could be my daddy," Sarah said brightly. "Then you could read me stories at night and—"

"Sarah!"

Eric turned to find Kate in the doorway, her face flushed.

"What's wrong, Mommy?" Sarah asked innocently, her eyes wide.

Eric watched silently as Kate drew a deep breath. "Nothing's wrong, honey. But you need to drink your soda so you can go to sleep. Then you'll be all better tomorrow, just like Dr. Eric said."

Eric stood as Kate moved into the room. She avoided his eyes, and bright spots of pink still burned on each cheek.

"I'll let myself out," he said quietly.

"No." She looked up at him, obviously still embarrassed by Sarah's remark, though good manners took precedence. "I put the kettle on. Please stay and have a cup of tea or coffee. And some cake. It's the least I can do after you came over here on your day off."

He hesitated, then nodded. "All right. I'll wait for you in the living room."

Kate watched him leave, then turned back to Sarah and helped her sit up enough to drink the soda.

"Are you mad, Mommy?" Sarah asked in a small voice.

"No, honey. Of course not."

"You seemed mad when you came back in the room."

Kate shook her head. "I wasn't mad, Sarah. I heard what you and Dr. Eric were talking about, and I just got sad for a minute because your daddy isn't here with us. He loved you very much, honey. Before you were born we used to plan all the things the three of us would do together. I'm just very sorry he can't be here to do them with us." Kate picked up the photo from the bedside table and gently traced Jack's face with her finger. "Don't ever forget how much he loved you, Sarah. He's part of you. See? You have his eyes. And you have that little dimple in your cheek, just like he had. So part of Daddy will always be with us in you."

Sarah studied the photo for a moment. "He was pretty, wasn't he, Mommy?"

Kate blinked to clear the sudden film of moisture in her eyes. "Yes, Sarah. He was very pretty."

"Do you think he misses us up in heaven?"

"I'm sure he does."

"But he can't come back, can he, Mommy?"

"No, honey."

"Do you think he would be mad if I got a new daddy sometime? Just for while I'm down here?"

Would he? Kate wondered, as she replaced the photo. She'd never thought of it quite that way. And in that context, she knew the answer. Jack wouldn't want Sarah to grow up without the influence of a kind, caring father in her life. They had always talked about how they wanted her to experience all the joys of a real family—two loving parents and at least a sibling or two. Jack would still want that, even if he couldn't be the one to provide it.

"No, Sarah," Kate replied slowly. "I don't think he'd mind. Your daddy would want you to have a father."

"But how would I get one?" Sarah asked, clearly puzzled.

"Well, I would have to get married again."

"Would you do that, Mommy?"

"I don't know, honey. Your daddy was a very special man. It would be hard to find someone like him again.''

''Is Dr. Eric like him?''

Kate glanced toward the bedroom door and dropped her voice. ''I just met Dr. Eric, honey. I don't know him well enough to answer that question.''

Sarah scooted down in the bed and pulled the covers up to her chin. Already her eyes were drifting closed. ''Well, then I think you should get to know him better,'' she declared sleepily.

Kate adjusted the covers, then reached over and touched the photo of Jack, her gaze troubled. For several long moments she just sat there. She didn't want to do anything that would diminish the love they had shared. It was a beautiful thing, and she would always treasure it in her heart. But it was only a memory now. And memories could only sustain one for so long.

Kate sighed as she reached over and turned off the light. Even if she was ready to move on—and she wasn't convinced that she was—Eric wasn't available. He'd made that eminently clear. In his mind, he still had a wife. And after his first disastrous marriage, he truly believed that medicine and marriage didn't mix. So, if and when she decided to consider romance again, she'd have to look elsewhere.

Except, for some strange reason that plan held no appeal.

Chapter Seven

Eric listened to the murmur of voices as he restlessly roamed around Kate's living room. He couldn't distinguish the words, but he could guess what they were talking about. Sarah's last remark had clearly embarrassed Kate. And probably upset her, as well. He suspected that she'd done everything she could to make Jack as real as possible for Sarah. But it was a hard thing to do when the little girl had no memory of him. To her he was only an image, like the characters in her storybooks, with no basis in reality. What she wanted was a real daddy—someone who could hold her hand and share her life. Kate was fighting a losing battle, Eric thought with a sigh. Sarah was too young to be comforted by stories of a father she had never known.

Eric wandered into the kitchen, shoving his hands into the pockets of his jeans as he glanced around. The room was small but homey, with several of Sarah's drawings displayed on the refrigerator. The remains of a hardly touched dinner lay strewn next to the sink—

macaroni and cheese, green beans, salad. Sarah must have started to feel badly before they ate more than a few bites.

His gaze swept over the eat-in counter that separated the living room and kitchen, taking in the pile of half-graded school papers, a copy of the church bulletin—and a loan statement at his elbow reflecting a balance of nearly six figures. Eric frowned and quickly glanced away. The latter was obviously private business. But he knew what the debt most likely represented: Jack's medical bills—probably for the extended-care facility where he'd spent his last months. Eric had seen too many instances where insurance covered only certain expenses in situations like that, leaving the survivors deep in debt. He could make a reasonable guess at Kate's salary, and he knew it would take her years to repay the loan. It just didn't seem fair, he reflected, his frown deepening as his eyes strayed back to the statement. He could write a check for the entire amount and not even miss it. To Kate, it was obviously a fortune.

"She's sleeping now."

Eric's gaze flew guiltily to hers and hot color stole up his neck. Kate glanced down at the counter, and a flush reddened her cheeks as she moved to gather up the papers, putting the statement at the bottom of the stack.

"Sorry. The place isn't usually so cluttered."

"I wasn't looking, Kate. It was just lying there," Eric said quietly. To pretend he hadn't seen the piece of paper would be foolish.

She sighed and her hands stilled, but she kept her eyes averted. "I know."

"For Jack's care, I assume?"

She hesitated briefly, then nodded. "The health insurance covered a lot, and the life insurance helped—later. But the expenses piled up so quickly. The debt was absolutely staggering. It still is. And with nothing to show for it," she added wearily, her voice catching in a way that tugged at his heart.

There was silence for a moment, and then she straightened her shoulders and looked up at him. "But you didn't come here tonight to hear about my problems. Let me get you that cup of coffee and cake I promised."

Actually, he wished she *would* share her problems with him. But he understood her reluctance. Their acquaintance was still too new. So he let it drop, nodding instead toward the sink. "It looks like you haven't even had dinner yet."

She glanced disinterestedly at the remains of the meal. "I had enough. I haven't been that hungry lately, anyway."

Eric frowned as she moved to the stove to fill the kettle, his gaze sweeping over her too-thin figure. "You can't afford to skip too many meals, Kate."

She shrugged as she set out two plates. "I eat when I'm hungry."

"Do you rest when you're tired?"

She paused in surprise, holding the knife motionless above the cinnamon coffee cake, and sent him a startled look. Then she turned back to her task. "I rest when there's time."

"Why do I think that's never?"

She turned to face him again, the smile on her face tinged with sadness. "You sound like my mother."

Eric didn't *feel* like her mother. Far from it. As his

gaze took in her ebony hair tumbling around her face, her dark eyes shadowed with fatigue, her slender, deceptively fragile-looking form, he felt a fierce surge of protectiveness sweep over him—as well as something else he tried to ignore. He cleared his throat.

"You're the only mother in this room, Kate. And father, too, for that matter. It can't be easy, raising a child alone, trying to play both roles."

Her eyes grew troubled, and she turned away to reach for the kettle as it began to whistle. "Listen, Eric, I'm sorry about what Sarah said. She has a way of coming out with things that aren't always...well, discreet."

He waved her apology aside. "Don't worry about it, Kate. I hear all kinds of things from kids. Most of it I don't take seriously."

She placed their cake on the counter, then reached for her tea and his coffee, pushing aside the school papers as she sat on a stool next to him.

"Looks like you have some work ahead of you," he commented, nodding toward the pile.

"That's the lot of a teacher, I suppose. A never-ending stream of papers to grade. I usually work on them after Sarah goes to bed so I don't have to give up any of my time with her."

He looked at her. She was seated only inches away from him—so close he could clearly discern the faint lines of strain around her mouth. "Does sleep enter into the equation anywhere?" he asked gently. "You look tired, Kate."

The concern in his voice touched her, and her throat tightened as an unaccustomed warmth swept over her. "I catch up on my sleep in the summer," she replied, striving for a light tone. The truth was, she needed to take a summer job as well, at least something part-time.

"I have a feeling you're the kind of woman who never gives herself a break."

She propped her chin in her hand and played with her tea bag, swirling it in the amber liquid. "Jack always said I was too intense," she admitted quietly. "That I took everything too seriously. But that's just the way I am. If I commit to something, I can't do it halfway. Like teaching. I didn't want to go back to it. I wanted to stay home with Sarah. But that wasn't to be. So as long as I have to work, I intend to give one hundred percent. The same with raising Sarah. I want to be the very best mother possible under the circumstances. That's why I spend every spare minute with her. It's why I grade papers and do lesson plans at night." She paused and looked over at him speculatively. "You strike me as being equally committed to your profession, Eric. I can't imagine you ever doing anything halfway."

He conceded the point with a nod. "You're right. But maybe that's not the best way to be. Sometimes I wonder if..." His voice trailed off and he stared down pensively into his coffee.

Kate knew he was thinking about his failed marriage, and impulsively she reached over and lightly touched his hand. The simple contact jolted him. "I have a feeling you're being too hard on yourself about...the past," she said quietly.

He stared down at her delicate hand as its warmth seeped into his very pores. It took only this simple innocent touch, filled with tender compassion, to remind him how lonely and empty his life had become.

That reminder left a feeling of bleakness in its wake. Carefully he removed his hand on the pretext of reaching for his fork.

"How did we get into such a heavy discussion?" he asked, forcing his lips up into the semblance of a smile as he speared a bite of cake.

"I don't know. I think we started off talking about food."

"Well, then, let's get back to that topic," he declared, "because this cake is wonderful. Did you make it?"

"Uh-huh."

He devoured another large bite, clearly savoring the dessert. "You know, the only time I ever have home baking anymore is at Mom's. I could live on this cake. What it is?"

"Sour-cream cinnamon streusel coffee cake," she recited with a smile. "It was one of my mom's favorite recipes. Kind of a family standard."

"Well, you can bake this for me anytime. I'd make more house calls if I always got treats like this in return."

"Do you actually make house calls?"

"Once in a great while."

"Well, I'm glad you did tonight. Although my checkbook might not be," she teased with a smile.

Eric stopped eating for a moment and looked at her. "There's no charge for this, Kate."

Her smile faded. "Wait a minute. This was a professional call, Eric. I expect to be billed. You don't owe me any favors. And I always pay my debts."

He finished off the last of the cake, then stood.

"Okay, then bake me one of these sometime and we'll be even."

"That's not..."

"Kate." He picked up his bag and turned to her. "I know you pay your debts. I saw evidence of that tonight. If you want to repay me, then do me a favor. Bake me one of these—" he tapped on the cake plate, then turned to look at her "—and get more rest. You're doing a great job taking care of Sarah. Now you need to take care of yourself."

She followed him to the door, prepared to continue the argument, but when he turned there was something in his cobalt-blue eyes that made her protest die in her throat. Their expression was unreadable, but the warmth in their depths was unmistakable. And when he spoke, his voice was slightly husky.

"Good night, Kate. Call me if Sarah isn't a lot better by tomorrow."

She swallowed, with difficulty. "I will. And thank you, Eric."

"It was my pleasure."

He looked at her for a moment, his gaze intense, and her breath got stuck somewhere in her chest. Slowly he reached up and touched her face, and she felt every muscle in her body begin to quiver. His fingers were gentle, the contact brief and unplanned, but as their gazes locked for an instant, Kate saw a flame leap to life in his eyes. Her stomach fluttered strangely, and she remembered Sarah's words to her earlier—*"I think you should get to know him better."*

Her mouth went dry and she seemed unable to move. Eric's gaze seared into her soul—assessing, discerning, seeking. She stopped breathing, not at all sure what was happening. Or if she could stop it. Or—most disturbing of all—if she even *wanted* to.

And then, abruptly, he turned away, striding quickly down the stairs. Kate stared after him, her heart hammering painfully in her chest as she thought about what had just happened. Had Eric been thinking about kissing her? Or had she only imagined it? But she hadn't imagined his touch. Her cheek was still tingling where his hand had rested.

And what did that touch mean? she wondered with a troubled frown as she slowly closed the door. And why had he done it?

Why did you do that? Eric berated himself as he strode angrily toward his car. He tossed his bag onto the passenger side and slid behind the wheel, his fingers gripping its curved edge as he stared into the darkness, struggling to understand what had just happened.

The self-control he'd carefully honed through the years had slipped badly tonight, he admitted. He wasn't normally an impulsive man. But as he'd looked at Kate's willowy form silhouetted in the doorway, he had been overwhelmed by a powerful urge to touch her, to reassure her in a tactile way that she wasn't as alone as she seemed to feel. He had wanted to tell her that she could always call on him, for anything. Had wanted to pull her into his arms and hold her. Had wanted to kiss her, to taste her sweet lips beneath his.

Eric let out a ragged breath and closed his eyes. Thank heaven he hadn't given in to that impulse; that he'd resisted his instincts and confined himself to a simple touch. But it hadn't been easy. And he had a sinking feeling in the pit of his stomach that the next time, it would be even more difficult.

Eric knew that he should strengthen his resolve to keep their contact to a minimum. He knew that just being around Kate was a dangerous temptation he didn't need. But he also knew it was a risk he was going to take—as soon as he regained his equilibrium and self-control. He figured that would take a week, maybe two. It wouldn't be easy to wait that long to see her again, he acknowledged. But he would manage it.

Three days later, Eric was already trying to think of an excuse to call Kate. So much for resolve, he thought grimly as he pulled into the attached garage of his modest bungalow, then headed down the driveway to retrieve the mail. She hadn't contacted him, so he'd assumed Sarah was feeling much better. Which had meant no more house calls. That was good, of course. For Sarah, anyway.

Eric reached into the mailbox and withdrew the usual assortment of bills and ads, flipping through the stack disinterestedly until a letter with his former sister-in-law's return address caught his eye. He frowned. Odd. He hadn't heard from Elaine since the divorce, more than four years ago. He closed the garage door and entered the kitchen, tossing the bulk of the mail on the counter and loosening his tie before slitting open the envelope and scanning the letter.

I know you will be surprised to hear from me, Eric, but I was reasonably certain that unless I wrote, you might never hear about Cindy. I know there was no love lost between the two of you by the time your marriage ended, but I think it's only right to let you know that she died a month ago. She was diagnosed with lung cancer a year ago—so far along that it was hopeless from the start. I guess her chain-smoking finally caught up with her.

Cindy never talked much about the divorce, although she did say that it was her idea. She was my sister and I loved her, but I want you to know that I always felt she had thrown away something pretty wonderful when she left you. I'm sure there was fault on both sides—there always is—but I suspect, much as I loved Cindy, that the bulk of it lay with her. I can only imagine what a devastating experience the breakup was for you, knowing what I do of you from contact during your marriage.

I hope life has treated you more kindly since the breakup, Eric, and wish you only the best in the future.

Elaine

Eric stared numbly at the paper, then slowly sat down at the table. Cancer was a devastating disease that ravaged its victims physically. He couldn't even imagine how Cindy, who had always taken such care with her appearance, had coped with that—not to mention all the pain and suffering that cancer inflicted.

For a moment he allowed himself to recall how she had looked at their wedding, her blond beauty absolutely radiant and perfect; and how his heart had been so filled with love on that dream-come-true day. But over the next few years he'd watched that dream slowly disintegrate, until the night of the accident, when it had become a nightmare.

Eric raised a shaky hand and raked his fingers through his hair. He hadn't thought about that night in a long time, had purposely kept the memory of their confrontation at bay. But now the scene came back with startling clarity, the sequence of events unfolding in his mind as if on a movie screen.

At Eric's insistence, they'd cut their evening short. He hadn't been able to get the accident out of his mind, and the smoke at the party had actually begun to make him feel nauseous. Usually he'd deferred to Cindy at such events, enduring them until she was ready to call it a night. But that evening he'd simply told her they were leaving. She'd fumed all the way home in the car, then had confronted him the moment they walked in the door, turning on him in cold fury.

"Okay, do you want to tell me what that caveman act was all about?"

Eric wasn't up to a fight. But her tight-lipped, pinched features and belligerent tone told him there was no avoiding a confrontation.

"I just couldn't handle it tonight, Cindy. Not after the accident. It all seemed so...shallow. And the smoke was making me sick."

She uttered an expletive that made him cringe. "Why do you have to take everything so personally, anyway?" she demanded harshly. "You did your best. More than you needed to, probably. Why can't you just walk away? It's only a job."

He thought of the accident scene, of the woman's devastated face, the man's mangled body. And of his wife's inability to understand, even after all this time, that walking away simply wasn't in his nature. "It's not that easy, Cindy," he replied wearily.

She reached for her purse and extracted a cigarette, staring down his look of disapproval defiantly as she lit it and inhaled deeply.

"You and I need to talk, Eric."

She was right. But he was too tired tonight for the kind of discussion she had in mind. "Tomorrow, Cindy."

"No. Now."

There was an odd note in her voice, and he looked at her with a frown. Her gaze flickered away from his, as if she was suddenly nervous, and his frown deepened. He suddenly felt sick again—not from the smoke, but from a premonition that whatever Cindy had on her mind was going to change their relationship forever. And he didn't want to hear it. Not tonight.

"Look, can't this wait?"

"No. It's waited too long already." She moved restlessly to the other side of the room, paused as if gathering her courage, then turned to face him.

"Eric, this isn't working anymore, if it ever did. You know that. Let's face it. This marriage was a mistake from the start. We're not a good match. You can't have enjoyed these last six years any more than I have."

Eric wanted to pretend that this wasn't happening. But the tenseness in his shoulders, the sudden feeling of panic, the hollowness in the pit of his stomach, made it all too real.

"We took vows before God, Cindy. We can't just toss them aside. Remember the 'For better, for worse'?"

She gave a brief, bitter laugh. "Oh, I know all about

the 'for worse' part. When do we come to the 'for better'?''

That hurt. There had been some moments of happiness, at least at the beginning. "We had some good times."

"A few," she conceded with an indifferent shrug. "But not enough to sustain this relationship. And I want more, Eric. In this marriage I'll always be competing for your attention with a bunch of sick kids. And I'm tired of losing."

"You knew I was a doctor when you married me."

She dismissed the comment with an impatient gesture. "I thought you were going to be a *surgeon*, Eric. With decent hours most of the time. Doing really important work. I didn't know you were going to turn into the pediatric version of Marcus Welby, always on call, always ready to jump every time some kid has a runny nose."

Eric's mouth tightened. Cindy had always made her opinion clear on the subject, but she'd never before used such hateful language.

Something in his expression must have registered, because when she spoke again she softened her tone. "Look, Eric, let's not make this any harder than necessary, okay? Let's just agree to call it quits and go our separate ways."

"You're asking for a divorce."

"Yes."

"Why now?"

She shot him an assessing look. "You want the truth?"

Suddenly he wasn't sure he did, but he nodded nonetheless.

She took a deep breath and reached down to tap the ash off her cigarette. "Okay. I've met someone I…like…a lot. There's potential there. And I want to be free to explore it." She paused, and as she watched the color ebb from his face, she spoke again. "I'm not having an affair, if that's what you're thinking. I wouldn't go that far, not while we're married. You know that."

He didn't know much of anything at the moment. He just felt shocked—and numb. He sat down heavily and dropped his head into his hands.

"Look, Eric, it's not that bad. Lots of marriages fail. This way we can both be free to try to find someone who is more compatible."

Slowly he raised his head, his face stricken, and looked at her. "I married for life, Cindy." His voice was flat, devoid of all emotion.

"I thought I did, too. But it didn't work out. I don't think God expects people to stay in miserable marriages."

"I think He expects people to try as hard as they can to make it work."

"I did try," she replied defiantly. "And it still didn't work. I'm sorry, Eric."

But she didn't sound sorry, he thought dully. She sounded almost…relieved. As if she'd made up her mind about this a long time ago and had been waiting for the right moment to tell him.

When he didn't reply, she glared at him impatiently. "So are you going to make this easy, or am I going to have to fight you on it?"

He raked the fingers of his hand through his hair and

his shoulders drooped. "I'm tired of fighting, Cindy. I can't hold you if you don't want to stay."

"Good." The relief in her voice was obvious. "I'm glad you're being sensible. It's for the best, Eric. Maybe you'll find someone in the future who'll make you a better wife."

He looked at her sadly. "I already have a wife, Cindy. We may be able to break the bonds of our marriage in the eyes of the law, but in the sight of God we'll always be married. 'Till death us do part.'"

Eric returned to the present with a start and stared at the letter from Elaine. "Till death us do part." The words echoed hollowly in his heart. He'd remained faithful to that vow, but the cost had been deep-seated loneliness and episodes of dark despair. Now he was free. He wasn't sure what that meant exactly. But there would be time to think about it later. Right now he needed to talk with the Lord. He closed his eyes and bowed his head. *Dear Lord, be with Cindy,* he prayed. *Show her Your infinite mercy and understanding. And forgive me for all the times I failed her. May she find with You the peace and happiness I couldn't provide her with in this life. Amen.*

Kate peered at the mailbox, verified the address, then pulled up to the curb and parked. She surveyed the small bungalow, surprised at its modest proportions and its location in this quiet, family-oriented neighborhood. She'd assumed that a successful doctor like Eric would live in more ostentatious surroundings.

She reached for the coffee cake, then paused as her nerves kicked in. She knew Eric hadn't really expected her to follow through on his "payment" suggestion for the house call. But it had given her an excuse to see him again. Just being in his presence made her feel good. In fact, since he'd come into her life she felt better than she had in a long time. Thanks to him, she was taking steps to renew her relationship with the Lord. Thanks to him, she'd found a wonderful care-giver for Sarah. And thanks to him, the spot in her heart that had lain cold and empty and dead for five long years was beginning to reawaken.

Actually, she wasn't sure whether to thank him for the latter. In fact she wasn't sure how to handle it—especially considering that Eric was off-limits. He'd made that very clear. Plus, she didn't know if she was ready to say goodbye to her past yet, despite Amy's advice. But something had compelled her to come here today. It might not be wise, but she had listened to her heart. She only hoped that it would guide her through the encounter to come. After their parting on Sunday night, Kate wasn't at all sure what to expect when Eric opened the door.

What she hadn't expected was his shell-shocked appearance. There were deep furrows between his brows, his hands were trembling and his face was colorless. She looked at him in alarm, her own trepidation forgotten as panic set in.

"Eric? What is it? What's wrong?"

He stared at her for a moment, as if trying to refocus. "Kate? What are you doing here? Is Sarah all right?"

"She's fine. I dropped her off at church for Christmas-pageant practice, and I wanted to stop by and re-pay you for the house call." She held up the coffee cake. "But…well, you look awful! Are you sick? What happened?"

He sighed and wearily passed a shaky hand over his eyes. "I had some...unexpected news. Come in, Kate." He stepped aside to let her enter, but she hesitated.

"Look, I don't want to intrude, Eric. Maybe I should come back another time."

"You're not intruding. And I'd like you to stay, actually. I could use the company."

Kate searched his eyes, but his invitation seemed sincere rather than just polite, so she stepped past him into the hallway.

"I was just going to make some coffee. Can I offer you some tea?"

"Thanks. But why don't you let me make it? You look like you should sit down."

He smiled wryly at her concerned expression as he led the way to the kitchen. "Don't worry, Kate. I'm not sick. Just shocked. But you look tired. Go ahead and sit down and I'll put the kettle on." He indicated a sturdy antique wooden table and chairs in a large bay off to one side of the kitchen.

She complied silently, watching as he stepped between the stove and the oak cabinets. He moved with an easy grace, a quiet competence that was restful and reassuring. She glanced around her. The kitchen was a lovely spot, cheerful and bright, with big windows that offered views of what appeared to be a large tree-shaded backyard. But the room itself was somewhat sterile, with few personal items other than a letter addressed to Eric on the table. Though Cindy had been gone a long time, Kate was surprised that there was so little evidence of the decorating touches usually initiated by the woman of the house. But the room was comfortable and clearly had great potential.

"I like your house, Eric," Kate remarked as he set plates and forks on the table.

"Do the honors on the cake, would you, Kate? And thanks. The house *is* nice. It's the kind of place I always wanted."

"Me, too. Jack and I had a house something like this when we first moved to St. Louis."

Eric heard the wistful tone in her voice, and it tugged at his heart. He knew from his mother that Kate had sold the house after Jack died. She'd needed the money for other things—like paying medical bills. But he didn't want her dwelling on the past.

"The only problem with this place is the decorating—or lack thereof. It needs to be warmed up, but I'm not even sure where to begin."

"I'm surprised Cindy didn't do more," Kate admitted.

"Cindy never lived here, Kate. I bought this place after the divorce."

"Oh. I'm sorry."

"No need to be. Believe me, this wasn't her style. We lived in a condo in West County when we were married. It was what she wanted, and it suited her."

But what about you? Kate wanted to ask. *Didn't your wants count? What about whether it suited you?* But she remained silent, for he suddenly grew pensive as his gaze came to rest on the letter. Kate suddenly realized that whatever it contained accounted for his recent shock. And that it had something to do with Cindy.

She looked over at him, and their gazes met. She

didn't want to pry, but she wanted him to know that she cared. "I'm a good listener, Eric," she said quietly.

He studied her for a moment, then sighed and turned away to retrieve their mugs. Kate tried not to be hurt by his silence. After all, they were recent acquaintances. She couldn't blame him for wanting to keep his problem private. But when he sat down he surprised her.

"That letter is from Cindy's sister."

Kate looked at him curiously but remained quiet.

"Cindy died a couple of weeks ago."

Kate stared at him in shock. Now she understood why he had looked so shaken when he answered the door. "What happened?"

"Lung cancer. I was always afraid her smoking would kill her."

"I'm so sorry."

He sighed. "I am, too. For her. For what might have been. For all the mistakes we both made. My strongest feeling at the moment is regret. It's odd, Kate. I have no sense of personal loss. No grief in that way. Cindy and I parted long ago, even before the divorce. By the end of our marriage we were really no more than strangers."

Kate couldn't imagine the living hell of that kind of relationship. She and Jack had had arguments on occasion, but deep down they'd always known that their marriage was rock solid, that it would endure, no matter what obstacles life put in their path. Eric had clearly never enjoyed that kind of relationship.

Impulsively she reached over and laid her hand on his, just as she had three nights before. "I'm so sorry, Eric," she repeated. "Not only for Cindy's death, but for the death of your marriage. In some ways, I think that would be even harder to bear than the physical death of a loved one. I was devastated when Jack died, but I had wonderful memories to cling to and sustain me. I'm sorry you never had that.''

Eric looked into Kate's tear-filled eyes and something deep within him stirred. It was such a foreign emotion that it took him a moment to identify it as hope. Here, with this special woman, he suddenly felt that his future no longer needed to be solitary and devoid of love. Which was strange. Because though he might now be free to marry in the eyes of the Lord, there were still major obstacles to overcome before he could even begin to consider a future with Kate. First of all, she was still in love with Jack. That was no small hurdle. And second, he was still a doctor, committed to a profession that didn't seem to mix with marriage— or at least, not for him. There seemed no way around that barrier.

And yet...Eric couldn't suppress the optimism that surged through him. It was as if a heavy burden had been lifted from his shoulders, as if the floodgates had opened on a parched field. Yes, the problems were significant. But all things were possible with the Lord. And maybe, with His help, out of the darkness of these past years a new day was about to dawn.

Chapter Eight

"So...I hear I have some competition in the baking department."

Kate took a sip of her tea and smiled at Anna. "Hardly."

"I don't know." The older woman's tone was skeptical, but there was a twinkle in her eye. "The way Eric raved about that coffee cake—it must be something special. It was nice of you to make one just for him."

"It was the least I could do after he stopped by to see Sarah—and on a Sunday night." Kate poured herself another cup of tea and sighed contentedly. "Mmm. This is the perfect antidote to a long, drawn-out teachers' meeting. Thanks for watching Sarah later than usual, Anna."

"My pleasure. She's a delightful little girl and no trouble at all." They simultaneously glanced out the window toward the patio, where the youngster was engrossed in some make-believe game, wringing every moment out of the rapidly diminishing daylight. "She's so excited about the Christmas pageant at church. It's all she's talked about for the last two days. If you need any help with the angel costume, I'd be more than happy to lend a hand."

Kate smiled and shook her head. "Speaking of angels—how did I get lucky enough to find you?"

"Well, you can thank my son for that. And it wasn't luck at all. It was just part of God's plan."

"What plan is that?" Kate inquired with a smile.

The doorbell rang before the older woman could reply. "Goodness! I don't usually have visitors at this hour," she remarked, a flush rising to her cheeks. "Will you excuse me for a moment, my dear?"

"Of course. We need to be leaving anyway." Kate started to get up, but Anna put a hand on her shoulder.

"Not yet!" There was an anxious note in her voice, and Kate looked at her curiously. Anna's flush deepened and she quickly backtracked. "At least finish your tea first," she said, before quickly leaving the room.

Kate stared after her, a sudden niggling suspicion sending an uneasy tingle down her spine. The older woman was up to something, she concluded. But what?

She had her answer a few moments later when Anna reentered the kitchen followed by Eric, who was toting two large white sacks.

"Well, look who stopped by," Anna declared, feigning surprise.

Kate sent her a chiding look, which the older woman ignored. Kate was beginning to realize that Anna was a matchmaker at heart and now seemed to be directing her efforts at her son and the mother of her young charge. Of course, she wouldn't get very far without the cooperation of said son, Kate reflected, directing her glance his way. And he wasn't in the market for romance. But as their gazes connected she somehow got lost in his blue eyes and warm smile and forgot all about conspiracy theories.

"Hi."

How did he manage to impart such a warm, personal tone to a single word? Kate wondered as she distract-edly returned the greeting.

He held up the sacks. "I heard you were working late tonight and thought maybe we could all share some Chinese. I brought chicken fingers and fries for Sarah."

Kate smiled, touched by his thoughtfulness. "She'll love that. It's not a treat she gets too often."

"How about you, Kate? Is Chinese all right?"

"Perfect. A treat for me, too."

Anna looked from one to the other with a satisfied expression. "I'll just call Sarah," she offered, heading toward the back door.

Kate rose to get some plates and eating utensils while Eric unpacked the bags. "You're going to spoil us, you know," she told him over her shoulder.

"You could use some spoiling."

She turned to him in surprise, and as their gazes met, a faint flush rose in her cheeks. There was some-thing...different about Eric tonight, she decided. She couldn't quite put her finger on it. He seemed less tense. Less worried. And definitely less distant. Which shouldn't surprise her, considering how much he'd shared with her Wednesday night about the deep-seated hurts and disappointments of his marriage. In fact, she'd been surprised by his openness. Most men she'd met kept their feelings to themselves—especially the

darker ones—as well as their doubts. Even Jack. Despite his outgoing nature, he'd had a hard time talking about feelings, preferring instead to express them.

But Eric had told her things that many men's egos would never have let them admit—his sense of failure when the marriage had faltered, his doubts about the compatibility of a family and his career, his sense of betrayal and deep hurt when Cindy had asked him for a divorce and told him she'd met someone new. It touched her deeply that he'd chosen to share his feelings with her. And as she'd left he'd looked at her as he had the prior Sunday, and had touched her cheek in just the same way.

Kate had thought about that evening a great deal over the last two days. She'd wondered what it meant, where it would lead. Now she was beginning to get a clue. Eric's visit tonight had clearly been planned. He was making an effort to see her, to get to know her better, to spend time with her. In other words, he was letting her know he was interested in her. At the same time, she sensed that he would wait for her to give him a sign that she wanted their relationship to move to a deeper level.

But Kate wasn't prepared to do that yet. She needed more time to sort through her conflicting emotions—and loyalties. With a self-conscious smile, she turned back to the cabinet and busied herself with the plates and glasses.

Eric got the message. Kate wasn't ready to cross the line from friendship to anything else yet. And frankly, he wasn't sure he was, either. So he would wait. And in time the Lord would show them both the way.

* * *

Somehow the Friday-night dinners became a regular event. So did Sunday church, with breakfast afterward. And Eric began calling her during the week to share amusing stories about his young patients and to ask about her day. Sometimes he would drop in unexpectedly for coffee, or sweep everyone off to an impromptu dinner out, much to Sarah's delight—not to mention her mother's.

Occasionally their evenings would be interrupted by Eric's pager, and though he always apologized, Kate assured him that she didn't mind. His deep compassion and fervent commitment to his work were part of who he was. To change that would be to change his very essence. And she liked him just the way he was.

By late October, he had become so much a part of their lives that the loneliness of the last five years began to recede in her mind until it was only a dim, unpleasant memory. In fact, not only did she begin to forget what life had been like before Eric, it was becoming harder and harder to imagine a future without him.

"Okay, partner, we need to have a talk."

Eric glanced up from his paperwork as Frank strode in with a determined look on his face, then dropped into the chair across from Eric's desk.

"What's up?" Eric asked mildly.

"We need to add a third physician to this practice," he declared without preamble.

Eric's eyebrows rose. "We've talked about this before."

"I know. And you were always reluctant. But that was when we were just getting established and *needed* to work twelve hours a day. We're past that now. We have a thriving practice. There's plenty of work for a third doctor. Plus, we'll only have to cover calls every third weekend instead of every two. With the baby coming, Mary thinks I need to lighten up my work schedule so I have more time to spend with the family. And I agree."

"So do I."

Frank opened his mouth to argue, stared at Eric, and shut it. "What did you say?"

"I said I agree."

"Just like that? No protest? No litany of reasons why this isn't a good time?"

"Nope."

Frank stared at him, his expression slowly changing from astonishment to smugness as the light dawned. "Oh, I get it. It's Kate."

"Kate?"

"Don't give me that innocent act. Of course it's Kate. Things are heating up, huh?"

Eric thought about their basically platonic relationship and smiled ruefully. "I wouldn't say that exactly."

"Oh, come on, buddy. You can tell me. Just because I haven't pestered you with questions about her lately doesn't mean I forgot the way you looked at her at the barbecue. I knew then something was in the wind. You're seeing her a lot, aren't you?"

"As a matter of fact, yes."

Frank grinned. "I thought so. Listen, I think that's great. It's about time you had something more in your life than a job and charity work. I'm glad for you, pal. This third partner will help us *both* out."

"Do you have someone in mind?"

"Absolutely. Carolyn Clark."

Eric knew her. She was one of the hardest-working pediatric residents he'd ever met, and her educational credentials were impressive. She'd be a good fit. "Is she interested?"

"Yep."

"Let's talk to her, then."

Frank shook his head incredulously. "You know, I thought I was going to have to do a real sell job on you about this."

Eric chuckled. "Not this time."

"So...I take it things are going well with Kate." Frank leaned back and crossed an ankle over a knee, clearly settling in for a long interrogation.

Eric looked at his friend speculatively as he recalled something his mother had said to him weeks ago about his partner's ability to balance marriage and medicine. He hesitated for a moment, then spoke carefully. "Can I ask you something, Frank?"

At the serious tone in Eric's voice, Frank straightened. "Sure. Shoot."

Eric steepled his fingers and sighed. "I guess it's no secret that Cindy and I made a mess of our marriage. And one of the biggest problems was my career. She hated how it intruded on our relationship and interrupted our private life. It was a major problem, and I just couldn't seem to solve it. If I had been able to, our marriage might not have fallen apart."

Frank's eyes narrowed. "It wasn't just *your* problem, Eric."

"What do you mean?"

Frank spoke slowly, obviously choosing his words

carefully. "Doctors' lives—whatever their specialty—don't belong completely to them. That's just the nature of the job. And good doctors—the ones who really care, who take the Hippocratic oath seriously—always serve two masters. Yes, we care for our families and the people we love. But we also have an obligation to do our best for the people we serve. Our patients' lives are literally in our hands. You don't have to marry a doctor to realize that. Cindy knew what she was getting into, Eric. Don't beat yourself up about that. She just wasn't willing to play second fiddle—ever. I think that reflects more on her than on you."

Eric wanted to believe Frank. But the doubts went too deep and were of too long a duration to be dispelled so quickly by his partner's reassurance. "What about you and Mary, Frank? How do the two of you deal with the demands? Doesn't Mary ever resent them?"

"Honestly? No. Which doesn't mean she isn't disappointed on occasion when my professional obligations interfere with our plans. But she accepts it as part of what makes me tick. And she knows I do everything I can to put her first the rest of the time and make time for us as a couple—like pushing for a third partner," he said, flashing a grin. "So we've never had any problems."

Eric looked at Frank silently for a moment, then sighed. "I wish I could be sure it worked like that for everyone."

Frank stood, his expression serious. "Don't let one bad experience stop you from having a good one, Eric. I don't know Kate very well. But I liked what I saw. Cindy's gone now. There's nothing except fear to keep you from moving forward. And let me say one more thing. You're just about the most conscientious, caring person I know. If you couldn't make a marriage work, nobody could. And if you ever tell anybody I got this mushy, I'll deny it,'' he finished with a smile as he exited.

Eric stared after him thoughtfully. He and Frank had been friends for a long time. Usually his colleague hid his deeper feelings under an umbrella of humor. But just now he'd spoken from the heart. Eric appreciated his flattering words, as well as his honesty. And Frank was right. He *was* afraid. Now the question was, could he get over those fears enough to take another chance on love?

Anna handed Kate another pin, then backed up and critically surveyed the hem of Sarah's angel costume. "I think that will do it. I'll run it up for you on the machine tomorrow, Kate."

Kate stood and lifted Sarah down from the sturdy kitchen chair, giving her a hug as she lowered her to the floor. "You're a beautiful angel, honey."

"Are we going to make the wings next week?" the little girl asked excitedly.

"Absolutely. Dr. Eric said he'd get some wire for us at the hardware store for the frame."

"Mommy's been working on the wreath for my hair at night after I go to bed," Sarah told Anna. "It's really pretty!"

"I think you'll be the loveliest angel there ever was," Anna declared with a smile. "Now let's get that gown off so it stays clean. Angels always look nice and neat, you know."

"I can't thank you enough for all your help, Anna,"

Kate said warmly when Sarah scampered off to play. "In a way, I feel that Sarah has a brand-new grand-mother."

"Well, it's a role I always wanted to play," Anna reminded her as she laid the gown over the sewing machine. "I love taking care of her. It's given me a new sense of purpose. I still miss Walter every day, of course, but it's easier to bear, somehow, knowing that you and Sarah are counting on me." She paused and turned to the younger woman. "And speaking of watching Sarah—I know this is rather short notice, Kate, but my cousin called last night. She and a friend were planning to go on a cruise the week of Thanks-giving, and her friend had to back out at the last min-ute. She asked me to go instead. I've always wanted to take a cruise, and this seemed like a providential opportunity. So I told her yes. But I'm afraid that means I can't watch Sarah on Monday and Tuesday of Thanksgiving week."

"Oh, Anna, don't give it another thought!" Kate assured her. "I'm thrilled for you! And Thanksgiving is still three weeks away. I have plenty of time to make other arrangements."

"Actually, I spoke with my neighbor—a lovely young woman, very responsible, with two small chil-dren of her own. Sarah's played with them on occasion. She said she'd be happy to watch her. I know you're leaving for your sister's Wednesday, and I'll be back Sunday night. So it's only for two days."

Kate was touched by the older woman's consider-ation. "Thank you, Anna. That sounds perfect," she said warmly. "And I hope you have a wonderful time on your cruise."

"Oh, I expect we will. Except..."

"Except what?" Kate prompted when Anna's voice trailed off.

"Well, I'm a little concerned about Eric. He'll be by himself on Thanksgiving, and I'm afraid it will be hard for him. It's always been the three of us on holidays. But when I spoke to him last night about the trip, he encouraged me to go and assured me he'd be fine. So I suppose I shouldn't worry. He'll probably go to Frank's."

Kate frowned. Eric wouldn't be spending the holiday with Frank because they were going to Mary's parents' house. He'd probably end up working the whole four-day weekend. Unless...

"Is something wrong, dear?" Anna asked, eyeing the younger woman with concern.

Kate forced herself to smile. "Not a thing." There was no sense mentioning the idea that had just popped into her head. Especially when she wasn't sure she would follow through on it, anyway.

"Hi, Amy."

"Kate? It's my Sunday, isn't it?"

"Yes. But Eric is stopping by in a little while, so I thought I'd just go ahead and call. Are you in the middle of something?"

"You mean other than the usual mayhem around this place?"

Kate chuckled. "What's going on now?"

"A friend of Cal's had to go out of the country on business for a few weeks and somehow conned my good-natured husband into baby-sitting his iguana. The twins are fascinated. Personally, when it comes to pets

I prefer the warm, cuddly variety. However, as long as I don't have to touch it, I suppose I can put up with a reptile in my house for a limited time. But speaking of 'warm and cuddly'—how are things with Eric?''

Kate flushed. She'd tried to downplay their relationship, but Amy wasn't inclined to buy the "just friends" routine. Which, in a way, might make it easier to broach the subject that was on her mind. "Things are fine."

"'Fine,' hmm. Would you define that?"

"I see him a lot. We go to church together and all of us eat dinner at his mother's every Friday night. Sometimes he drops over. Like tonight."

There was silence for a moment. "Look, Kate, I don't want to pry—or push. So if you want to tell me to mind my own business, it won't hurt my feelings in the least. But is it really just a friendship thing with you two?"

Kate played with the phone cord. "Yes. Although sometimes I... Well, I think maybe he'd like for it to be more. I mean, I know he still has concerns about mixing medicine and marriage. He got burned pretty badly the first time he tried that. So he's gun-shy. But I have a feeling if I gave him some encouragement he might be willing to at least...consider it."

"And I take it you haven't?"

"No. I'm still trying to put my own past behind me," Kate admitted, her gaze coming to rest on the wedding picture that hung over the couch. "It's really hard to let go, you know? Even after all this time."

"Yeah, I know." Amy sighed. "I guess you just need to listen to your heart and do things at your own pace, Kate. You'll know when it's the right time to move forward."

Kate took a deep breath. "Actually, that's one of the reasons I called. I think maybe it *is* the right time. At least to take a few small steps." Kate explained Anna's Thanksgiving plans and her concern about Eric being alone. "So I wondered if maybe... Well, I thought that—"

"Invite him," Amy interrupted promptly.

"Honestly?"

"Of course. One more mouth to feed in this household won't even be noticed. And there's plenty of room. We'll kick out the iguana if we have to."

Kate laughed. Amy had always had a knack for making her feel better. "You're a pretty terrific sister, you know that?"

"Just paying back an old debt. Seems to me you were a pretty good sounding board once when I really needed guidance. If it wasn't for you I might never have married Cal and ended up living in the heart of Tennessee. You know, come to think of it..."

Kate smiled at her teasing tone. "You wouldn't trade your life for anything and you know it."

"You're right about that. Listen, you bring that overworked doctor down here and we'll show him a Thanksgiving he won't forget."

"Thanks, Amy."

"My pleasure. Just do me a favor, okay? Warn him about the iguana."

Kate didn't mention the holiday that night when Eric stopped by for cake and coffee. In fact, it took her a whole week to work up the courage to broach the subject. And when she did, it was at the last minute, as he walked Sarah and her to the door after Sunday services.

Kate fitted her key in the lock and ushered Sarah inside, then turned to Eric, struggling to get her suddenly-too-rapid pulse under control. "Thanks again for the ride. And for breakfast," she said a bit breathlessly.

"You're welcome."

Though there was a chill in the early-November air, his smile warmed her all the way to her toes. "Uh, Eric…"

He looked at her curiously, alerted by something in her tone. "Yes?"

"I'm glad your mother is going on that cruise."

"So am I. It will be a nice change of pace for her. She sounds like a kid when she talks about it—which is most of the time. I didn't think we'd get a word in edgewise at breakfast today."

"I know. She's so excited! But… Well, what about you? It won't be much fun to spend the holiday alone."

He shrugged dismissively. "I'll be fine."

"Your mom is kind of concerned about you being by yourself."

He tilted his head and eyed her quizzically. "Did she tell you that?"

"Uh-huh."

He frowned. "I told her not to worry."

"That's how mothers are. It's in the job description." She paused and took a deep breath. "To be honest, I'm not too happy about the situation, either. So I thought you might like to… Well, I talked to Amy and…you know we always go there for Thanksgiving, and there's plenty of room—Amy said so. Except she did tell me to warn you about the iguana. Cal's watch-

ing it for a friend of his. Amy's not too happy about
that, but the kids love it and—'' Her nervous babbling
ceased abruptly when Eric laid his hand on her arm
and gazed down at her.

''Kate, are you asking me to spend Thanksgiving
with you and your family?'' he asked quietly.

She swallowed with difficulty and nodded. ''Listen,
I know it's kind of a long trip and they're all strangers
to you, so it's okay if...''

''I accept.''

She looked at him in surprise. ''Really?''

''Really. Because between you and me, I *wasn't*
looking forward to spending this holiday alone. And I
can't think of anywhere I'd rather be on this Thanksgiving than with you. And Sarah. And Amy and her
family...and the iguana,'' he teased, a twinkle
springing to life in his eyes.

Kate's gaze was locked on his, and she watched,
mesmerized, as the twinkle suddenly changed to an em-
ber that quickly ignited, deepening the color of his
eyes. Her breath caught in her throat as he slowly
reached over and touched her face, letting his hand
linger before gently raking his fingers through her hair.

Though the touch was simple, its effect on Kate's
metabolism was anything but. She longed to lean
against his solid chest, to feel his arms protectively and
tenderly enfold her. She closed her eyes and sighed
softly, instinctively swaying toward him.

Eric read her body language, recognized the invitation she was unconsciously issuing, and fought down
the sudden urge to pull her close. *Dear Lord, give me
strength,* he prayed, his heart hammering in his chest.
He wanted to hold her tightly, to touch her, to caress

the soft waves of her ebony hair and the silky smoothness of her cheek. He wanted to press his lips to hers and taste their sweetness. Bottom line, he wanted a whole lot more than he *should* want at this point, he reminded himself as he struggled to control his desires. Get a grip, admonished himself sharply. This is not the time. Or the place.

With a triumph of willpower that surprised him, he dropped his hand and stepped back, drawing a long, shaky breath as he did so.

Kate opened her eyes and blinked, as if trying to clear her vision, then reached out to grip the doorframe as she stared at him.

"I'll call you," he promised, his gaze locked on hers.

She nodded jerkily. "Okay." It was barely a whisper.

He held her gaze for a moment longer, then with obvious effort turned and strode quickly away. Not until he was out of her sight did he pause for a moment to take a deep, steadying breath. He knew that Kate was close to reaching out to him. The real question now was whether they were both ready. During the last couple of weeks he'd thought a lot about his conversation with Frank, and he was gradually beginning to believe that maybe…just maybe…marriage and medicine could mix—with the right woman. Namely, Kate. But even if he resolved his own issues, there was still Jack. Could she let him go? And could she ever find it in her heart to love someone else as intensely as she'd loved her husband?

Eric wasn't sure. And that uncertainty left him discouraged. For if he truly set out to win the heart of this special woman, he realized he could face a daunting task. The simple fact was, his experience in dealing with *living* rivals was extremely limited. And he was at a total loss about how to deal with a dead one.

Chapter Nine

Kate glanced over her shoulder at Sarah, whose excited chatter had finally been silenced by sleep, and smiled. Her gaze connected with Eric's as she turned back, and he glanced briefly in the rearview mirror, his own mouth lifting at the corners.

"Looks like the sandman finally won."

"Thanks for being so patient, Eric. I'm sure you would have preferred a quieter drive."

"Honestly? No. Most of my drives are far *too* quiet. This was a nice change."

"Well, Sarah isn't usually this wound up. It's just that she's been so excited about the trip. She was up at dawn, ready and waiting."

"Which means her mother was up at dawn, as well."

She shrugged. "I had things to do anyway."

"You must be tired, Kate. Why don't you grab a nap, too?"

The sudden tenderness in his voice made her stomach flutter, but she tried to ignore the sensation. "I'm okay. The fact is, I'm excited, too. I've been looking forward to seeing Amy and her family as much as Sarah has. The kids are cute, Cal is great and Amy... Well, Amy's special. I hope you like her, Eric."

"I'm sure I will. Especially if she's anything like you."

She felt a warm flush rise to her face. "Actually, we're pretty different," she replied, striving to maintain a conversational tone. "Amy has always been more outgoing and self-confident, sort of a take-charge kind of person—in the best sense of the term. She's a doer and an organizer and always has things under control. Unlike me."

Eric frowned and glanced over at her. "I think you're selling yourself short."

Kate gazed unseeingly into the deepening dusk. "'Control' isn't a word I would apply to my life in recent years," she said quietly.

"The things that happened were *beyond* your control, Kate," Eric reminded her gently but firmly. "You coped admirably under extremely difficult circumstances and through it all you've been an exceptional mother. That ranks you pretty highly in my book."

Kate turned to study his strong profile, trying unsuccessfully to read his expression in the dim light. "I have a feeling you're just being kind, Eric, but in any case, thank you."

His gaze flickered momentarily to hers. "I'm not just being kind, Kate. Trust me."

That tender, intimate quality was back in his voice, and her heart stopped, then raced on. "You know, Dr. Carlson, you're going to turn my head with all these compliments. Pretty soon I'll have to add conceitedness to my list of faults,'' she quipped, unwilling yet to deal with the implications of his flattery—and his tone. She was relieved when he picked up on her cue and responded with a chuckle.

"Why do I doubt that?" he countered.

They lapsed into companionable silence then, and by the time they pulled into the drive that led to Amy's log house it was after ten. The crunch of the tires on the gravel announced their arrival, and as they pulled to a stop, the front door was flung open to reveal a silhouetted, jeans-clad figure.

Kate smiled softly. "Amy's been watching for us."

Before Eric could respond, the woman in the doorway called something over her shoulder, then raced down the steps, bypassing the last one with a leap. Kate pushed open her door, and the two women met in front of the car, clinging to each other in a fierce hug.

"Oh, Kate, it's so good to see you!" Amy said fervently.

When Kate replied there was a trace of tears in her voice. "I've missed you so much!"

Eric leaned against the car and folded his arms across his chest as he silently watched the reunion. Though it was difficult to see much in the dim light, there were definitely some physical differences between the two women. Amy was taller than Kate, and her hair wasn't nearly as dark. While Kate was softly rounded in all the right places, Amy's build seemed more angular and athletic. And her movements suggested a more boisterous, impulsive nature than Kate's. But whatever their physical or personality differences, it was clear that the sisters shared a strong emotional bond. He felt touched—and honored—that Kate had included him in this family gathering.

When Amy at last extricated herself from the hug, she strode toward him and extended her hand. "You're obviously Eric. Welcome."

He straightened quickly and took her fingers in a firm grip. "And you're obviously Amy. Thank you for inviting me. I'm looking forward to being part of your holiday."

Amy tilted her head and planted her hands on her hips. "I hope you still feel that way when you leave on Sunday. Kate did tell you about the iguana, right?"

He smiled. "I've been duly warned about your temporary guest."

"Well, I'm glad you used the term 'temporary,'" she confessed with relief. "We're eccentric enough without having strangers think we regularly keep weird animals in our house. You'll be happy to know that Wally isn't sleeping in your room."

"'Wally'?"

"The iguana." She rolled her eyes. "An iguana named Wally, can you believe it? The next time Cal agrees to—"

"Did I hear my name mentioned?"

A tall, dark-haired man slipped his arm around Amy's shoulders and she turned to look up at him. Her expression softened, though her tone was teasing. "You did. We were discussing Wally."

Cal grimaced good-naturedly. "Why do I think I'll never hear the end of this?"

"Because you won't," she replied pertly. "But enough about Wally for the moment. Eric, this is my husband, Cal. Cal, Eric Carlson."

While the two men shook hands and exchanged greetings, Amy slipped from under Cal's arm, peered inside the car and grinned. "Looks like someone nodded off."

"About a hundred and fifty miles ago," Kate informed her.

"Well, I'm sure you're all exhausted after that long drive. Are you hungry?" She glanced from Kate to Eric, and they shook their heads.

"We stopped for dinner along the way," Kate told her.

"Okay. Then let's get you all to bed. We can visit tomorrow."

By the time everyone was settled, it was nearly eleven. Sarah and the twins were happily rolled into sleeping bags in the living room, while Kate took the twins' room. Eric was assigned the sleeper sofa in the den.

"Now, is there anything else you need tonight?" Amy asked.

"We're fine," Kate assured her. "Get some rest yourself."

Amy chuckled and glanced at her watch ruefully. "Fat chance. Believe it or not, Caitlin still likes a midnight bottle. My six-month-old," she explained to Eric.

He smiled. "A healthy appetite is a good sign."

"I'll remind myself of that while I'm feeding her in the wee hours," she replied with a wry grin. "Good night, you two."

They watched her disappear up the rough-hewn split-log stairway, and then Eric turned to Kate. The warmth in his eyes banished the evening chill. "Sleep well," he said huskily.

She opened her mouth to reply, discovered she'd somehow misplaced her voice, and forced herself to take a deep breath before trying again. "I usually do when I'm here. I like being in the country."

"I do, too. This seems like a perfect spot to celebrate an all-American holiday. Thanks again for inviting me, Kate."

She smiled. "Like Amy said, save your thanks until we leave. It can get pretty crazy around here with all the kids."

"It's a good kind of crazy, though."

Her smile softened. "Yeah, it is."

Kate expected him to turn away then, but instead he propped a shoulder against the doorframe and shoved his hands into the pockets of his jeans. He drew a deep breath, and in the dim light of the hall Kate could see twin furrows etched between his eyes.

"Is something wrong?" she asked in concern.

He glanced down at her, and his frown eased. "No. I'm just thinking how nice it is to be in a home so obviously filled with love. Amy and Cal seem to have created something really special in this house. I can feel it, even in the short time I've been here. It's heartwarming to see such a successful marriage."

"They do happen, Eric. I know."

He looked down into her eyes and nodded slowly. "I know you do. I guess the question is…"

His voice trailed off, and Kate felt her breath catch in her throat. She could guess what he was thinking, and she knew she ought to leave his comment alone. But she spoke anyway. "The question is what?" she ventured hesitantly.

Eric gazed at her for a long moment. Then, instead

of replying, he withdrew one of his hands from his pocket and reached over to cup her chin, his thumb stroking her cheek. It was a casual, uncomplicated gesture. But the warmth of his gentle touch, the compelling look in his eyes, turned it into so much more. A deep yearning surged through Kate, and she felt her heart pause, then race on. She wanted more, she realized. She wanted him to hold her in his strong arms, to tenderly claim her long-neglected lips. Instinctively Kate knew Eric's briefest kiss would transport her to a land of emotion from which she had long been estranged.

Eric saw the longing in Kate's eyes and could no longer ignore—or suppress—the attraction that sparked between them. It was time to test the waters. Slowly he leaned toward her, his gaze locked on hers. His own pulse was none too steady, and he closed his eyes as their lips came whisper close, eager to taste the sweetness of—

"Oh, I'm glad you're both still up. I forgot—"

Kate heard Eric's sharply indrawn breath and pulled back, startled. She felt hot color suffuse her face as she turned to her sister.

Amy paused on the bottom step and quickly assessed the situation. "Uh, listen, leave it to me to barge right in at the wrong time. I just wanted to let you know that we planned to go to services tomorrow morning at ten, if that's okay with you two."

"Th-that's fine. Thanks." Kate tried unsuccessfully to control the tremor in her voice.

"So…good night again. This time for good," Amy promised as she made her way up the stairs. A few seconds later a door very deliberately clicked shut.

There was a long moment of awkward silence. Then Kate wrapped her arms around her body and tried to smile. "Amy always did have impeccable timing," she said shakily.

Eric let out a long breath and raked the fingers of one hand through his hair. "That's for sure."

"Listen, it's getting late anyway. We're both tired. Maybe...maybe we should just call it a night."

He looked down at her for a moment, the haze of desire still evident in his eyes. Finally he sighed and nodded. "I guess you're right. But remember one thing." His voice was husky as he reached over and touched her cheek.

"Wh-what?" she stammered, her gaze locked on his.

"To borrow a line from *Gone With the Wind*, 'Tomorrow is another day.'"

And with that enigmatic comment, he turned and disappeared down the hall.

Tomorrow was, indeed, another day. But it was a family affair—from the pancake breakfast to the church service to the dinner preparations, when everyone was recruited to help. Eric found himself peeling potatoes after Amy slapped a paring knife into his hand and said she figured if he could handle a scalpel, he could handle that.

The meal itself was a joyous, boisterous affair, and afterward everyone pitched in on the cleanup. They paid their respects to Wally, admired the gazebo Cal was building in a grove of rhododendrons at the back of the property, and stayed up late, reminiscing and playing board games. The next day was equally busy, and the evening not conducive to privacy—Amy was up till all hours with a fussy Caitlin. On Saturday Cal took them into Great Smoky Mountains National Park for a "VIP tour," as he laughingly called it.

"This isn't the best time of year for the park, but it has its beauty in all seasons," he told them as they wandered down a particularly lovely path by a crystal-clear stream. As the children ran ahead, and Cal and Amy strolled arm in arm, Caitlin sleeping—finally!— in the carrier on Cal's back, Eric slowed his pace and turned to Kate.

"Alone at last," he declared with a grin.

She gave him a wry glance. "Hardly."

"Why do I think this is as good as it's going to get while we're here?"

Kate looked up at him apologetically. "It's been a bit overwhelming, hasn't it? I'm sorry, Eric. I guess I didn't realize that—well, that you were hoping for some time alone."

He reached over and deliberately laced his fingers with hers. A tingle ran down her spine at his touch, and she felt warm color rise in her cheeks when he spoke. "I guess I didn't, either—until the night we arrived. As you've probably realized by now, I tend to be the slow-moving, cautious type when it comes to relationships. Maybe too much so. At least that's what Frank says."

Kate smiled understandingly. "I'm the same way. Just ask Amy. I like to be sure about things, and some-times…sometimes that holds me back."

"I know. Unfortunately, life doesn't seem to offer many certainties."

"Maybe…maybe there are times when you just have to trust your heart."

He looked down at her, his eyes serious. "I haven't been willing to do that for a long time," he admitted honestly.

She gazed up at him, searching his eyes, wanting to ask the question that hovered on her lips but feeling afraid to do so. Yet he seemed to read her mind, and answered it.

"I've felt…differently about a lot of things since I met you, Kate," he told her quietly.

"So…so have I," she confessed haltingly. "But I'm still not sure about what to do. Reverend Jacobs has been really great, though, in helping me sort out my feelings. And I've been following his advice to pray for guidance."

He smiled and squeezed her hand. "Since I've been doing the same thing, why don't we leave it in the Lord's hands for the moment? He'll show us the way in His own time."

She nodded. "I think that's a good plan. But can I tell you something?" she added impulsively. "I hope He doesn't wait too long."

Eric chuckled. "You and me both."

"Okay, I put Cal in charge of Caitlin's midnight feeding and very firmly told him that it was now or never for our sister-to-sister tête-à-tête. Here's your hot chocolate. Let me throw another log on the fire and then we're all set," Amy said briskly.

Kate tucked her feet under her and smiled as Amy joined her on the couch a moment later. "This is nice."

Amy sighed contentedly and nodded. "Yeah, it is,

isn't it?'' She settled herself comfortably into the cushions and took a leisurely sip of her hot chocolate, then turned to find Kate grinning at her. ''What's wrong?''

Kate chuckled and reached over to wipe the sticky marshmallow mustache from her sister's upper lip. ''It's nice to see that some things never change,'' she teased.

Amy grinned impudently, but a moment later her face grew melancholy. ''Too bad other things do, though,'' she reflected wistfully.

Kate's expression sobered. ''You're thinking about Mom, aren't you?''

''Yeah. It seemed so strange not to have her here for Thanksgiving. It's like a puzzle with a missing piece. She was always such a rock. No matter what scrapes I got into, I could always count on her to get me back on the straight and narrow, or to point me in the right direction when I was lost. Now I feel kind of like a ship adrift without an anchor. And on top of everything else, I missed her gravy at dinner. No one made it like Mom.''

Kate nodded. ''I thought about that, too.''

''It must be doubly hard for you, Kate,'' Amy reflected with a frown. ''She was part of your everyday existence. I can't even imagine the gap her death left in your life.''

Kate blinked back her tears and turned to gaze into the fire. ''It was pretty awful. Sometimes, in those first few weeks, I'd get so lonely… You'll think I'm crazy when I tell you this, Amy, but there were times I actually talked out loud to Mom. Like she was still there. Meeting Anna has helped a lot, though. It's not the same as having Mom, of course, but in many ways she reminds me of her. And she's taken Sarah and me under her wing. It was a godsend that she came into our lives when she did. I was grieving so much for Mom and at my wit's end about the day-care situation. Then she just appeared, out of the blue. I'll never get over it."

"The timing was pretty incredible," Amy concurred. "I'm glad you met her. And Eric, too." She took a sip of her hot chocolate and then spoke carefully. "I know you insist that your relationship is pretty platonic, but I have to say things didn't look like 'just friends' the other night when I interrupted you two."

Kate blushed and gazed down into her mug. "I think maybe it won't be platonic for much longer," she admitted quietly.

"Can I say I'm glad?"

Kate looked at her curiously. "Why?"

"Because I like what I've seen of Eric these few days. Because Sarah obviously adores him. And most of all because I think it would be good for you to let love back into your life. The question is, are you willing to open that door?"

Kate nodded slowly. "I think so, Amy. In fact, I think I'm... Well, I think I'm falling in love with Eric. But I still love Jack. Sometimes I feel so confused. I mean, how can I love them both?" she asked helplessly.

"How does a mother love more than one child? The heart has an infinite capacity for love, Kate. We can love many people in our lives, all in different ways. The love you have for Jack will always be there. Part of your heart will be his and his alone until the day you die. But that doesn't mean there isn't room for someone else. Love Eric for himself—for all the special qualities that are uniquely his. That won't diminish in any way the love you have for Jack. It's just different. A new dimension of love, if you will.''

Kate reached over and took Amy's hand. In the firelight her eyes shimmered with tears. "Thank you, Amy.''

"For what?''

"For understanding. For trying to help me find a way to let go.''

Amy squeezed her hand, and when she spoke her voice was slightly unsteady. "It's time, Kate. In your heart I think you know that. And I have a feeling that one very special doctor is waiting for you to close the door on the past and open the one that says Future. Because until you do, things will go nowhere. There's no place for him in your past. But unless I'm way off the mark, I think he'd very much like to be part of your future.''

Kate glanced toward the passenger seat and her lips curved up into a tender smile as she gazed for just a moment at that very special doctor, who was now sleeping quite soundly. In repose his face looked younger, more relaxed, more endearingly vulnerable. Reluctantly she turned her attention back to the road. Though she'd insisted they take her car for the trip, he'd been equally insistent about driving them down. But for the trip back she'd convinced him that they'd both arrive more rested if they took turns. She'd even encouraged him to sleep on this final lap, and he'd taken her up on it. In fact, both of her passengers had drifted off.

Absently Kate switched on her wipers as a soft drizzle began to fall. She was actually glad to have some quiet time to think. Since her conversation with Amy the night before, she'd felt a new sense of peace and resolution. Everything suddenly seemed more clear. Months before, when her pediatrician had retired, she could have chosen any number of doctors as a replacement. But she'd selected Eric, a man who had once saved her husband's life. Though some would dismiss it as an odd twist of fate, Kate believed there was more to it than that. Things happened for a reason. The Lord had guided her toward Eric, and through him, to Anna. Both had enriched her life tremendously. And now it seemed that she was being given the chance to find love once again. The choice about whether to pursue it was hers; but the opportunity had come from the Lord. And, with His help, she resolved to start building the future Amy had referred to.

The rain intensified, and Kate's full attention snapped back to the road. Ever since the accident five years before, she'd hated driving in bad weather, especially at night, and avoided it whenever possible. But she could handle a little rain, she told herself encouragingly.

Twenty minutes later, however, when the rain turned to sleet, her confidence faltered. As the small ice particles zinged against the windshield, she frowned worriedly and tightened her grip on the wheel. She detested sleet. It brought back the nightmare of the accident with harrowing intensity. Her heart began to thump painfully, and she risked a quick glance at Eric, who was still sleeping soundly. She knew he'd take over in a minute if she asked him to, but she hated to wake him. He worked too hard and slept too little as it was. And she wasn't at all sure he'd gotten much rest on this trip, between the sleeper sofa and Caitlin's night-time fussiness. She glanced at her watch. They were less than an hour away from home. She could do this if she took it a mile at a time, she told herself firmly. Her fears were irrational, after all. She had to get over them sooner or later. She might as well take the first step tonight.

Eric wasn't sure exactly what awakened him. But as he slowly came back to reality an odd noise registered in his consciousness. He frowned, struggling to identify the sound. Once he opened his eyes, the icy buildup on the windshield quickly gave him his answer. Sleet. His gaze flickered to the road. Judging by the glaze, the freezing rain had been coming down for some time.

Eric quickly straightened and turned to Kate. Though the car interior was dim, the tension in her body was evident in her rigid posture and white-knuckled grip on the wheel. She was driving slowly and cautiously, with absolute concentration, and seemed completely oblivious to everything but the task at hand. These conditions must be a stark reminder of a similar night five years before, he realized, suddenly filled with compassion.

"Kate." He spoke softly, trying not to startle her, but she jumped nonetheless as her gaze jerked toward his.

"Oh! You're awake." Her voice sounded tight and was edged with panic.

"How long has the weather been this bad?" he asked with more calm than he felt. It was obvious that he needed to get her out from behind the wheel as quickly as possible. She was terrified. The hazardous conditions had clearly brought back the traumatic memories of the accident.

With a hand that shook badly, she reached up and tucked a strand of hair behind her ear. "About...about half an hour."

"Why don't you pull onto the shoulder and let me take over?" he suggested quietly.

"It's too icy to stop here. And there's...there's a drop-off at the edge." There was a note of hysteria in her voice now.

"There's plenty of room, Kate," he reassured her soothingly. "Just take it slow and easy. There's no one behind us. I'll help you." He placed his hand protectively over hers on the wheel, alarmed by her frigid fingers. "Come on, sweetheart, just guide it over real gently. That's right."

With his help she edged the car halfway onto the shoulder. Eric glanced into the rearview mirror as they rolled to a stop, and was relieved that there were no other vehicles in sight. "Can you just slide over here, Kate? I'll go around to the driver's side."

Jerkily she nodded. By the time he'd slipped and slid around the front of the car and settled himself behind the wheel, she was huddled into the passenger seat. Her face was totally devoid of color, a thin film of perspiration beaded her upper lip and her breathing was shallow. He frowned as he reached over to take her cold hands in his.

"Kate?" She turned to him, her eyes slightly dazed. "Everything's going to be fine. We're almost home. You'll be back in your apartment in less than an hour. Okay?"

She nodded mutely.

He released her hands reluctantly. What he wanted to do was take her in his arms until her trembling ceased. But he suspected the best way to calm her was to get her out of the car and into her apartment.

The remaining drive was made in silence, though he glanced her way frequently. She stared straight ahead, her hands clenched in her lap, her posture still rigid. And, in truth, her concern—if not its intensity—was valid, Eric admitted. The roads were slick and hazardous, and continued to worsen as the minutes passed. He didn't realize how tense *he* had become until they pulled into a vacant spot in front of her apartment and he shut off the engine. Only then did the knotted muscles in his shoulders and the tension in his neck register. He took a deep breath and turned to Kate.

"Home at last," he said quietly.

Shakily Kate reached up and brushed her hair back from her face. "Th-thank you for driving, Eric. I'm sorry you had to take over."

"I didn't mind, Kate. I just wish you'd woken me up sooner."

"Are we home?" A sleepy voice from the back seat interrupted them.

Eric turned, lightening his tone. "Indeed we are, Miss Sarah."

She rubbed her eyes and stared out the window. "Oh! It's snowing!"

"Not yet. But it wouldn't surprise me if we didn't wake up to a winter wonderland tomorrow. Right now it's just ice. And very slippery. So I'm going to carry you up to the apartment, okay?"

"Okay. Can I build a snowman tomorrow if it snows, Mommy?"

Eric glanced at Kate. "Your mommy's awfully tired right now, honey. She drove for a long time. We'll decide about the snowman tomorrow." He turned to Kate and reached over to rest his hand on her knee. "Sit tight, okay? I'll take Sarah in and come back for you."

"I can manage, Eric."

"Humor me, okay? I don't think we want any trips to the emergency room for broken bones on a night like this."

He had a point. "Okay." She reached for her purse and fumbled around for her keys.

He squeezed her shoulder as she handed them over, then opened his door and carefully stepped out. The pavement was like a newly cleaned skating rink, he concluded, moving with extreme caution as he reached in for Sarah. "Hold on tight, sweetie."

He was back more quickly than Kate expected, his collar turned up against the pelting sleet. "Take it slow and easy, Kate," he cautioned as he opened her door and held out his hand. "Walking is pretty treacherous."

She took his hand and stepped out, steadying herself on the car door. "What about the luggage?"

"I'll come back for it. First I want to get you inside where it's safe and warm."

She didn't argue. At the moment, anywhere safe and warm sounded like heaven.

Eric kept a firm grip on her arm as they made their way slowly up the steps from the parking lot and along the walk. He was right—the night was too dangerous for either walking *or* driving, she reflected. Not until she'd stepped inside did she finally relax, her shoulders drooping as she drew a weary sigh.

"I've never been all that thrilled with this apartment, but right now I could get down and kiss the floor," she admitted, summoning up a shaky smile.

"I have a better idea." He took her hand and led her to the couch, then gently urged her down. "Sit for a minute and take a few deep breaths. You'll feel a lot better. I'll get the luggage and then head back to my place before it gets any worse."

"But Eric, it's too dangerous to drive!" she protested in alarm.

"Why can't Dr. Eric stay here tonight, Mommy?" Sarah piped up. "He can sleep on the sofa bed, just like you used to do before Grandma went to heaven."

Kate looked up at Eric. His eyes were unreadable. "Would you consider it?" she asked uncertainly. "I'll be so worried if you try to drive home. It's not safe out there."

Eric studied her. She seemed so vulnerable, her eyes huge in her white face, her body still trembling, her dark hair loose and mussed around her face. She was right about the danger outside. But suddenly he was a whole lot more worried about the danger inside.

Chapter Ten

The sudden whistling of the kettle bought him a moment's reprieve. "I put the water on to boil when I brought Sarah in," he said over his shoulder as he headed for the kitchen. "I figured you could use a cup of tea. Let me make it and then we can discuss the situation."

Except what was there to discuss, really? he thought as he mechanically pulled a mug from the cabinet and added water and a tea bag. The weather was terrible. It didn't make sense to take risks. But what about the risks right here? he countered silently. Kate was an extremely desirable woman. He'd been attracted to her for weeks. So far, past experience and a conviction that marriage and medicine didn't mix had allowed him to exercise some discipline in their relationship. But this weekend he'd almost kissed her. And though Amy's untimely interruption had effectively derailed his passion, the desire was still there. It might not be wise to stay. But common sense told him that venturing out again tonight would foolish.

With sudden decision he picked up the mug and stepped out of the kitchen, frowning as he glanced around the deserted living room. A moment later, Sarah's girlish giggle, followed by the low murmur of voices, echoed down the hall and he headed in that direction.

Kate looked up guiltily when he entered Sarah's bedroom. "I know you asked me to wait, but I wanted to get Sarah into bed as quickly as possible. It was a long trip for her."

He handed her the mug, noting the lingering quaver in her hand. "It was also a long trip for her mother," he replied quietly. "Go on back into the living room and relax. I'll put Sarah to bed."

"Oh, goody!" the little girl exclaimed, clapping her hands. "Will you read me a story, too?"

"A short one, if you get your pajamas on really quick."

As she scampered down the hall to the bathroom, Kate looked up at Eric. "Are you sure you don't mind doing this?"

"Not in the least. Go back out there and put your feet up. Doctor's orders," he added, flashing her a grin.

She rose slowly. "Listen, Eric, I'm sorry Sarah put you on the spot about staying tonight. And I understand if you don't want to. But the weather is so bad and..."

He reached over and gently grasped her upper arms, effectively stilling her voice. "I'm staying, Kate," he said deliberately. "I was just taking a minute to...think about it."

His gaze was locked on hers, and Kate stared up at

him silently, certain he wasn't referring to the weather. A swarm of butterflies suddenly took flight in her stomach.

"Oh. Well, okay. I'll...I'll be in the living room."

And then she fled.

At first, as Kate waited for him to join her, she sat perched on the edge of the couch, her shoulders hunched nervously, her hands tensely gripping the mug. But as she slowly sipped the soothing liquid and listened to the voices in the back bedroom—Sarah's high and excited, Eric's deep and mellow—she gradually began to relax. It was an odd feeling, to let someone take care of *her* for a change and help her with her daily chores, she mused. And it suddenly occurred to her that she could get used to this.

But she had better not, she warned herself. After all, the man had never even kissed her. Not that he hadn't tried, she conceded, her lips curving up into a smile. It was ironic that Amy, who had been the one urging her to put some romance back in her life, had also been the one to derail Kate's first romantic encounter in years.

Eric had thrown her the classic line from *Gone With the Wind* as they'd parted that night. Was tonight the "tomorrow" he'd referred to then? she wondered, as a warm surge of adrenaline shot through her. It had been such a long time... She wasn't even sure she remembered *how* to be amorous. Her only consolation was that Eric was equally rusty. She shook her head ruefully. They were quite a pair.

"Want to share the joke?"

Startled, Kate looked up to find Eric smiling at her from the doorway. She tried vainly to stifle the flush that rose to her cheeks, desperately searching for a truthful but evasive response.

"I was just thinking about...about Amy."

"Hmm." She wasn't sure he believed her, but fortunately he let it pass. "Let me get a cup of tea and I'll join you."

She scooted over to make room for him, noting as she placed her mug on the end table that her hands were once again trembling. She clasped them together tightly in her lap and took several long, deep breaths. This was ridiculous, she scolded herself. After all, she was a grown woman. She could handle this situation. Okay, so maybe she was a little out of practice. But if she just remained calm, she'd be fine. Eric was probably just as nervous as she was, she told herself consolingly.

Except he didn't look in the least nervous as he settled down comfortably beside her, she noted enviously. In fact, the man looked totally relaxed.

"Feeling better?" he asked.

She nodded stiffly. "Uh-huh. The tea helped a lot. Thank you."

"My pleasure." His gaze swept over her face appraisingly. She did look better now, he decided. There was more color in her cheeks and the dazed look had left her eyes. "I'm just sorry you had to go through that."

She sighed, and her eyes grew troubled. "You'd think after all these years I'd have gotten over my fear of being in a car in bad weather. But I can't seem to shake it. Even here in town I try to avoid driving when the roads are slick. Especially at night. Sometimes I have to, of course, but it always shakes me up."

"I noticed."

She flushed. "It's so embarrassing. I feel like I should be able to put that night behind me and move on. But I can't seem to get past it."

Eric draped an arm loosely over her shoulders and gently massaged her stiff muscles. "Don't apologize, Kate. You weren't just involved in a fender bender. It was a nightmare situation. That kind of trauma can linger for years. In fact, you may never get over it completely. You'll probably always be extra careful in winter-weather driving—which isn't necessarily a bad thing, by the way. But eventually the fear should subside to a more manageable level. There's no need to rush it. Things usually happen in their own time."

His reassuring comments and the soothing touch of his hand went a long way toward easing Kate's tension. She sighed and relaxed against his arm.

"That feels good," she murmured. "I guess I was more tense than I realized."

He set his cup on the coffee table. "Turn around and I'll do both shoulders."

She did as he instructed, angling herself on the couch so that her back was to him. With a gentle but firm touch he massaged her shoulders, her upper arms, her neck, until the tension at last evaporated.

"Has anyone ever told you that you have great hands, Doctor?" she asked languidly, dropping her head forward.

Eric stared at her slender shoulders, at the dark hair spilling over his fingers, and drew a deep breath. "Not lately," he replied, his voice suddenly husky.

Kate heard the different nuance in his tone and felt

her pulse quicken as his touch changed subtly from therapeutic to sensual.

"You have beautiful hair, Kate. Has anyone ever told *you* that?"

"Not lately," she echoed breathlessly.

Slowly she drew in her breath and held it as he combed his fingers through her hair. A moment later a jolt of electricity shot through her when she felt his lips on the back of her neck.

"You taste good, too," he murmured.

Kate closed her eyes and uttered a small, contented sound deep in her throat as he moved her hair aside and let his lips travel across the full width of her neck. "Oh, Eric," she breathed. "I'd forgotten how good this could feel!"

"Me, too." He turned her then, urging her to face him with gentle hands on her shoulders. Their gazes connected, and she could see the fire smoldering in the depths of his eyes. "But I'd like to remember," he continued. "And I'd like to make some new memories. With you."

She stared at him, mesmerized by the profound emotion and honesty she saw reflected in his eyes. Her throat contracted with tenderness. "I'd like that, too," she whispered, and was rewarded with a smile that warmed her through and through. Slowly he reached over to touch her face, but stopped when she backed off slightly.

"What's wrong?" he queried in concern.

She blushed self-consciously. "It's just that I'm...I'm really out of practice. And I guess I'm a little bit afraid that I won't be...that you won't like... I haven't kissed a man in years, and I feel so awkward and schoolgirlish and— Boy, I'm really blowing this, aren't I?" she finished artlessly.

Eric's expression eased and he chuckled. "Can I tell you something? I have exactly the same fears. So what do you say we both just relax? I have a feeling everything will turn out fine."

Kate forced her trembling lips into a smile. "If you say so."

He reached out to her again, and this time she remained still, letting her eyelids drift closed as his fingers made contact with her skin.

Eric moved slowly, taking time to savor the feel of her skin beneath fingertips that were suddenly hypersensitive as he traced the sweet contours of her face, memorizing every nuance. She felt so soft—so good. He knew that they were breaking new ground in their relationship tonight; knew that there was no turning back once they started down this path. And part of him was still afraid. The wounds from his first marriage had left scars that ran deep. But somehow he sensed that with Kate, things would be different. He'd prayed for guidance, had asked the Lord to give him the courage to trust his heart, and so now he stood poised at a crossroads: he could either stay on the safe, predictable, lonely path he'd been following, or move in a new, uncharted direction that could bring love. The choice was his.

He gazed tenderly down at Kate's upturned face, at the soft fanning of her dark lashes against her cheeks. There was a fineness to her; a goodness that radiated from deep within. It wasn't in her nature ever to be hurtful or selfish or inconsiderate. He knew that as surely as he knew the sun rose in the east. She was a kind, caring woman who had shown great courage and endurance in the face of tragedy. She was also a loving and conscientious mother. And though she had strayed from her faith for a time, she had eventually found her way home again.

And then there was her beauty. With her flawless complexion, lovely features and slender, toned body, she looked closer to twenty-five than thirty-five. And her hair—it was soft and full and made for a man's hands to tangle in, he thought, combing his fingers through the wavy tresses.

In short, she was an incredibly desirable woman.

And yet…she'd remained alone for five long years, true to the memory of her dead husband. That, too, he admired in her. Loyalty and enduring love were qualities to be respected and honored. He knew she was still struggling to reconcile the possibility of a new relationship with her devotion to Jack, and was reluctant to do anything that diminished the memory of their love and commitment. So he felt deeply honored that she was willing to open her heart to him. Not to mention deeply attracted. Until Kate, he hadn't so much as *considered* the option of falling in love again. Now it wasn't just an option; it was a very real possibility.

Eric let his other hand drop to her waist and closed the distance between them. He felt her begin to tremble again, and he knew she was afraid, just as he was. Where would this lead? Were they making a mistake? Would they both end up hurt? Eric didn't know. But there was only one way to find the answer to those questions. Taking a slow, deep breath, he leaned toward her and tenderly claimed her lips.

Though his touch was gentle, Kate was momentarily stunned by the electric sizzle that shot through her. At the same time, she felt as if she'd been waiting for this moment for years. And maybe, in a way, she had. There had always been physical affection in her life— as a daughter, a mother, a sister. But this kind of affection had long been absent. And she'd missed it. A sweet shiver of delight swept over her and her heart soared with an almost-forgotten thrill as Eric's lips moved tenderly over hers, igniting long-dormant desires deep within her. Without consciously realizing what she was doing, she put her arms around his neck and pulled him even closer.

Eric was momentarily taken aback by her complete surrender to his embrace and by her ardent, uninhibited response. He'd expected her to be tentative and uncertain. Instead, she was giving herself fully and willingly to the kiss. And he was delighted. Because it meant that she not only cared for him, but also trusted him. And he had no intention of betraying that trust.

Kate felt his firm, sure hand on her back, through the thin fabric of her turtleneck. She could feel the hard, uneven thudding of his heart. She could feel his ragged breath. But most of all she could feel his lips, hungry yet tender. And she responded willingly, reveling in the embrace of this wonderful, caring man.

At last, with obvious reluctance, he drew back enough to gaze down at her.

She stared up at him, able to utter only one, breathy word. "Wow!"

His lips tilted up into an unsteady, crooked grin. "Yeah. Wow!"

She touched his face wonderingly, hesitantly reaching out to trace his lips with her fingertip. His sudden, sharp intake of breath made her pause, and she started to withdraw her hand. But he grasped it and held it firmly in place.

"Don't stop," he said hoarsely, closing his eyes.

Slowly she continued her exploration, her fingertips memorizing the planes of his face. Only when she'd finished did he open his eyes. He held her gaze compellingly as he lifted her hand to his lips and kissed the palm.

This time it was her turn to gasp. He paused and raised his eyebrows questioningly.

"Don't stop," she murmured, echoing his words.

He kissed each fingertip before enfolding her hand protectively in his, his fingers warm and strong around hers. Then he drew a long, ragged breath. "You know what you said earlier, about being out of practice?" he reminded her with a crooked grin. "If this is what you're like when you're rusty, I have serious concerns for my blood pressure when you're up to speed."

She blushed and smiled shyly. "I guess I got a little carried away."

"Hey, I'm not complaining! I just didn't expect things to get so...intense...so quickly."

"Me, neither."

"Are you sorry?" His tone was serious now, his face concerned.

She considered the question for a moment, finding it hard to concentrate when one of his hands was stroking her nape and the other was entwined with hers. "No. I think in my heart I realized at some point that this was inevitable. And we're not exactly strangers on a first date. We've known each other for over three months, Eric. This evolution of friendship into romance—well, it feels right to me. And natural. And comfortable. Not to mention…exciting.'' Her face grew warm, and he gave a relieved chuckle.

"I'm glad you added that last adjective. For a minute, there, I was beginning to feel like a pair of old slippers," he teased.

She smiled. "'Old slippers' is hardly the way I would describe you. More like a pair of fancy shoes I once bought—classy and sophisticated and guaranteed to make a woman feel drop-dead gorgeous and desirable.''

"Well, you're definitely all of the above. And I plan to do everything I can to make you feel that way every day from now on.''

Kate looked up at him, and the tenderness in his eyes made her throat constrict with happiness as her heart soared with hope. For the first time in years she began to think that maybe, just maybe, she wouldn't spend the rest of her life alone.

The smell of freshly brewing coffee wafted into the bedroom, slowly coaxing Kate awake the next morning. But even though the aroma was appealing, she fought the return to full consciousness. She wanted to hold on to this lingering, inexplicable feeling of contentment—most likely a remnant of some already forgotten dream—for just a little longer.

But she couldn't ignore the knock on her door a few minutes later. And she especially couldn't ignore the husky male voice that accompanied it.

"Are you decent?"

Her eyelids flew open and she stared at the ceiling

in shock. The feeling of contentment *wasn't* an illusion, after all. It was as real as the man standing on the other side of her door. She struggled to a half-sitting position and frantically pulled the blanket up to her neck, clutching it against her chest with both hands as her pulse skyrocketed.

"Y-yes. Come in."

Eric opened the door, a coffee mug in one hand, and paused for a moment to smile at her. His gaze, intimate and tender, lingered on her face, then did a leisurely inventory of the dark mass of hair tumbling around her shoulders, the demure neckline of her gown, the cheeks still flushed from sleep. With her wide eyes, slightly parted lips and endearingly modest posture, she looked vulnerable...and beautiful...and very, very appealing.

With a jolt that rocked him to his core, Eric suddenly realized that he wanted to wake up beside this special woman every morning for the rest of his life. But how could things have progressed so quickly? he wondered in confusion. When he'd claimed Kate's lips last night, he'd considered it a first step down a new path in their relationship. Yet he now realized that it hadn't been a first step at all. It had simply verified what his heart had known for weeks. He was in love with her. But was he ready for that kind of commitment?

And then she smiled—a tentative, endearing smile that tugged at his heart and chased away his doubts. Yes, he *was* ready, he realized. Maybe past ready. But he wasn't so sure about her. Though she'd responded fully to his overtures last night, she might be having second thoughts in the light of day. He knew she still had issues to deal with, and he couldn't push her. But he also knew with absolute certainty that one day in the not-too-distant future he would ask her to be his wife. It was just a matter of waiting for the right time.

"Hi, Mommy." Impatient about the delay in seeing her mother, Sarah squeezed past Eric and plopped on the bed beside Kate.

Lost in the intensity of Eric's gaze, Kate needed a moment to refocus and respond. "Hi, sweetie. Do I get a good-morning hug?" She leaned over to kiss her daughter, holding her close for a long moment as she willed her breathing to calm. She glanced at the clock as she released Sarah, and her eyes grew anxious. "Oh, no! I forgot to set the alarm last night. I'll be late! I've got to get up!"

Eric moved beside her and placed a hand on her shoulder. "Your school declared a snow day. You're a lady of leisure today."

Her posture relaxed and she drew a deep breath. "It must be pretty bad out there. They never call snow days."

"It is."

He handed her the coffee, and she gave him a warm smile. "Thank you. I'm not used to such service. Do you do windows?" she teased.

He chuckled and gave her a wink. "Depends what the job pays."

She flushed but was saved from having to reply when Sarah spoke up.

"Are you staying here all day, Dr. Eric?"

"I wish I could," he declared regretfully. "But kids still get sick when it snows. So I need to go and take care of them."

Kate looked at him worriedly. "What are the roads like?"

He shrugged. "Manageable in daylight. The radio said the main routes are clear and I'll be careful, Kate," he promised gently, reaching out to touch her cheek.

She swallowed. "Okay."

"I'll call you when I get to the hospital."

She gave him a grateful look. "Thank you."

"Take it easy today, okay? Get some rest."

She nodded mutely.

He hesitated, then turned to Sarah. "Do you think you could find a piece of paper and a pencil for me in the kitchen, honey?"

"Uh-huh." She scooted off the bed and skipped down the hall.

As soon as she was out the door, Eric looked back at Kate. "I enjoyed last night," he said huskily.

"So did I."

"And I couldn't leave without doing this." He leaned over, and her lips stirred sweetly beneath his promise-filled kiss. "I wish we had more time," he admitted. His breath was warm on her cheek as he reluctantly broke contact.

"There's always tonight."

He gazed down at her with a warm, amused smile. "Is that an invitation?"

"Yes."

"I accept."

At the sound of running feet, he quickly turned to the doorway.

"Is this okay, Dr. Eric?" Sarah asked, holding out a tablet and pencil as she reentered the room.

"That's perfect, honey." Eric took it and scribbled something, then handed it to Kate. "That's my pager number, just in case you need me."

Her spoken reply was a simple, "Thank you," but in the silence of her heart another voice responded differently. "I'll always need you," it said.

For a moment, Kate was taken aback by those words. Though they were simple, too, their implication was not. And suddenly she knew that the time had come to put her past to rest. Only then could she give herself a chance at a future that included this very special man.

Kate climbed onto the kitchen chair she'd dragged into her bedroom and carefully withdrew a box from the top shelf of her closet. As she deposited it in the living room, she glanced at the clock. Sarah had gone to the park down the street with the little boy next door and his mother, which meant Kate had about an hour to herself. That should be plenty of time, she decided, as she made herself a cup of hot chocolate and put on the CD of classical music that Amy had given her last Christmas.

Kate settled herself comfortably on the couch, took a deep breath and lifted the lid of the box. The familiar cream-colored envelope on top produced the usual melancholy pang, though it wasn't quite as intense this year. She fingered the envelope gently, then withdrew the formal invitation. As her eyes scanned the conventional wording, she found it hard to believe that eleven years ago today she had walked down the aisle as a radiant bride. So much had happened since then. So much had changed. In many ways, she felt like a different person. The youthful girl in white, so optimistic, so filled with dreams for the future, so deeply in love with her husband-to-be, seemed almost like a stranger, or a character in a story she had read—not actually lived.

She set the invitation aside and reached for the album, pausing to take a sip of her hot chocolate as she flipped open the first page. It was an annual ritual that she and Jack had begun on their first anniversary. They would usually open a bottle of champagne and slowly work their way through the photos, sometimes laughing, sometimes stopping to kiss, sometimes pausing to offer toasts. She'd continued the tradition after his death, substituting hot chocolate for the champagne.

When Kate reached the last page—a close-up portrait of the two of them—her eyes misted as her gaze lovingly traced Jack's handsome, dear face. He had been a wonderful husband. There had been no one else like him—no one who touched her heart in quite the way he had, no one who had his knack for making her find that special place inside herself where the child still lived. And there never would be again. She knew that with absolute certainty. And she accepted it.

With Reverend Jacobs' help, she had also accepted Jack's death, had made her peace with the Lord's decision to call him home sooner than either of them had expected. She felt ready, at last, to move forward with her life—and her relationship with Eric. Much of the credit for that went to Amy, who had put into words what Kate had begun to feel in her heart: that her love for Eric in no way diminished what she and Jack had shared. That time in her life—those memories—stood apart and belonged always to them. She and Eric would create something new that was theirs alone, touch places within each other that no one else had ever touched. They would move forward together, leaving doubts and guilt behind, and face tomorrow with hope.

Suddenly Kate remembered the counted-cross-stitch sampler she'd worked on at Jack's beside during the months he'd been in the long-term nursing facility. With a frown, she tried to recall where she'd put it. Somewhere in her closet, she was sure. A few minutes later, after rummaging around on the floor, she emerged triumphantly with a dusty bag. She waited until she was seated again on the couch before she carefully withdrew her handiwork and gazed at the partially stitched words from Jeremiah. She read them once, twice, a third time. They had given her hope as she'd sat by Jack's side, she recalled, but she'd bitterly put the sampler away unfinished—just like her life—after he died.

Kate looked again at their wedding portrait on the last page of the album, and her throat tightened with emotion. For she knew that this ritual, which had helped sustain her during the last few years, was now coming to an end.

"I love you," she whispered, her voice catching. "I always will. You were my sunshine, Jack. You filled my life with joy and beauty and laughter. I'll never forget that. And I'll never let Sarah forget what a wonderful father she had in you. But it's time now for me to let you go. I know you're with the Lord, and that you've found the contentment and wholeness that only comes when we are one with Him in heaven. But I still have a road to travel here. And I don't want to make the journey alone. I think Eric is going to ask me to marry him soon, and I'm going to accept. He's a wonderful man. You would have liked him, I think. And it's my most fervent prayer that you'll always know I love you no less because I also love him." She paused as her eyes misted with tears. "Goodbye, my love. Until we meet again."

And then, very gently, she closed the album.

Chapter Eleven

"I'll get it!" Sarah called as she raced from the living room to the front door.

Kate smiled and wiped her hands on a dish towel. It might have taken *her* a long time to figure out where Eric fit in the scheme of things, but for Sarah, who had no memories holding her back, he had immediately meshed seamlessly and naturally into their lives.

"Hi, sweetie. Did you build a snowman today?" she heard Eric ask.

"Yes. Mark and me and his mommy went to the park and made a gigan—gigan—really big snowman with a carrot for a nose and charcoal for eyes."

Kate liked the sound of his chuckle—deep, rich and heartwarming. "Now that sounds like a first-class snowman. Did your mommy go, too?"

"No. She said she had stuff to do."

Kate stepped into the living room then and smiled at Eric. The snow had started up again, and delicate white flakes clung to the shoulders of his dark wool

coat. He looked rugged and masculine, she thought, as
her heart skipped a beat.

"Hi."

He glanced up to return her greeting, but the words
died in his throat. She looked absolutely radiant tonight, he thought in awe. On a peripheral level he noticed her deep blue angora sweater and black stirrup
pants, and her hair, brushed loose and full, lying softly
on her shoulders. But it was the glow on her face that
stunned him. For the first time in their acquaintance
she seemed truly relaxed and at ease, he realized. There
was a profound calmness, a serenity about her that
reached out and touched his very soul. Something
about her had changed—and changed dramatically—in
the hours since he'd reluctantly left her to enjoy her
snow day. It was as if an event of great significance
had occurred. But what?

Kate saw the sudden look of speculation on his face
and flushed. Was her newfound inner peace so obvious? But Eric was a perceptive man. She should have
realized he'd immediately sense the change in her, just
as she should have realized that he'd quickly notice the
changes in the room, as well. In one quick, discerning
sweep his gaze passed over, then returned to the spots
where photos of her and Jack had once been displayed.

Sarah's powers of perception were none too shabby,
either, Kate acknowledged wryly. The little girl was
watching the proceedings with interest, and quickly
noted the direction of Eric's glances.

"Do you like our new picture?" she piped up.

His brain was so busy trying to process the significance of Kate's redecorating efforts that it took a moment for the question to register. When it did, he trans-

ferred his attention from the Monet print behind the
couch to Sarah. "It's very pretty."

"I like it, too," she declared. "It was in the hall
closet. Mommy said it was too pretty to keep hidden
away. So she took the wedding picture down. She said
sometimes you have to put things away to make room
for new things."

Eric turned to Kate, whose cheeks were tinged with
warm color.

"Mommy let me put the picture from the TV in my
room, too," Sarah continued, oblivious to the intense
atmosphere. "She said we're going to get some tulip
bulbs in pots to put there instead, and that we can
watch them grow all winter. She said they'll help us
keep spring in our hearts even when it's cold and snowing outside. Isn't that right, Mommy?"

Eric's gaze remained locked on hers. "That's right,
honey," Kate replied unsteadily, reaching up distract-
edly to push her hair back from her face. And that was
when Eric noticed the most significant thing of all.

The ring finger of her left hand was bare.

"Aren't you going to say hi to Mommy?" Sarah
demanded when the silence between the two adults
lengthened.

Once again, it took him a moment to collect his cha-
otic thoughts. "Of course I am. In fact, I'm going to
do better than that." His gaze never leaving Kate's, he
closed the distance between them, hesitated long
enough to give her time to protest, then leaned over
and kissed her.

"Hi," he greeted her huskily, one hand resting
lightly at her waist. "I missed you."

"We missed you, too," Sarah added. "But Mommy said you'd be back."

"Mommy was right."

"We're having chicken and dressing and biscuits tonight," she announced. "And chocolate cake!"

"And broccoli," Kate reminded her daughter.

"Sounds like a celebration. Broccoli and all," Eric remarked.

Kate's flush deepened and she turned toward the kitchen, trying to steady her staccato pulse. "Sarah, you have just enough time to finish watching your video before dinner."

"Okay." The little girl happily returned to the TV set and sat down, cross-legged.

As Kate walked toward the counter, she was aware of Eric close behind her. And she wasn't at all surprised when he placed his hands on her shoulders and leaned close, his breath warm on her neck.

"I like the redecorating."

She took a deep breath as she turned to face him, and he looped his arms loosely around her waist. They were only inches apart, and she felt lost for a moment in the depths of his deep blue eyes. "It was time," she replied quietly.

"You're sure about this?"

She nodded. "I don't want to live in the past anymore, Eric. I'll never forget my life with Jack. And I'll always love him," she added honestly. "But memories can only sustain you for so long. I've tried to hold on to them, but as a result I've ended up putting my *life* on hold. I've felt like a hollow, empty shell for too long. There was a time when my life was rich and full

and filled with promise. I want to feel that way again.
I want to move forward and make new memories.''

She didn't say, ''With you,'' but somehow she had
a feeling he knew what was in her heart. And his next
words not only confirmed that, but sent her hopes soaring.

He reached over and tenderly cupped her face with
his strong, capable hands. ''I feel the same way, Kate,''
he told her huskily. ''What do you say we start making
those memories together?''

Kate couldn't remember a Christmas season so filled
with joy and breathless anticipation. For once she
didn't mind the cold weather, and moved with renewed
energy and a lightness of step. Her daily chores, for-
merly dreary, no longer seemed burdensome and endless. Because always, at the end of her day, there was
Eric. Whether it was a simple dinner at her apartment
or an impromptu meal out, whether it was a ''family
outing'' with Sarah and Anna, or quietly sipping hot
chocolate with Eric by the tree after Sarah went to bed,
each moment was golden. And Kate treasured every
single one, storing them in a special place in her heart
reserved just for Eric. Their relationship, so long purely
friendship, blossomed rapidly into a genuine romance.

Once, Kate paused in surprise as she passed a mirror,
hardly recognizing for a moment the woman with the
sparkling eyes, flushed cheeks and animated face who
stared back her. She shook her head and smiled ruefully. There was no hiding it, she admitted. It was there
for all the world to see. She was in love.

Even Sarah noticed. As Kate tucked her daughter
into bed one night after Eric had been summoned to

the hospital for an emergency, the little girl suddenly looked up at her, her expression quite serious.

"Are you going to marry Dr. Eric?" she asked solemnly, without preamble.

Kate's heart stopped, then tripped on. She'd been expecting this question, but she still wasn't sure how to answer it—or the others that would inevitably follow. Slowly she sat down on the bed and took Sarah's hand, silently asking the Lord for guidance.

"He hasn't asked me yet, honey."

"But what if he does?" she persisted.

"Well, what do you think I should do?"

She considered for a moment. "Would he live with us if you got married?"

"We'd all live together. Probably at Dr. Eric's house."

"Would he be my daddy?"

This was the tough one. Kate struggled to find the right words—words that would keep Jack's memory alive but leave room for Eric, as well. "Actually, Sarah, you'd have *two* daddies." She reached over and picked up the photo of Jack. "When you were born, this was your daddy. He's in heaven now, so you can't see him, but he still loves you very much. And so does Dr. Eric. He'd be your daddy here. So you see how lucky you would be? You'd have a daddy in heaven and one here on earth."

"Do you still love my first daddy?"

Tears pricked her eyes, and Kate swallowed. "Of course, honey. I always will. He was very special to me. But he wouldn't want us to be lonesome. And I know he'd like Dr. Eric. I think he would probably be very happy if Dr. Eric took care of us, since he can't be with us himself.''

Sarah thought about that for a minute. "You know something, Mommy?" she said at last.

"What, sweetheart?"

"I would really like to have a daddy I could see. If Dr. Eric asks you to marry him, I think you should. Then we could be a real family. And that would be my best Christmas present ever!"

As Kate bent over to kiss Sarah, her heart gave a silent, fervent reply.

And mine as well.

"Kate? Eric. Listen, I've got a problem at the hospital."

Kate frowned and glanced at her watch. Sarah had to be at church in forty-five minutes for the Christmas pageant, and Eric had planned to take them.

"Kate?" Eric prompted when she didn't reply.

"I'm here. Will you be tied up long?"

She heard his weary sigh over the line. "Possibly. I've got a little boy who was just diagnosed with meningitis."

Kate's throat tightened and she closed her eyes. She'd read stories about the dangerous, fast-moving illness. "Oh, Eric! I'm sorry. How old is he?"

"Seven. Even worse, he's an only child. The parents are panic-stricken."

"How bad is he?"

"Bad."

She swallowed. The tone of his voice said everything. "Listen, don't worry about tonight, okay? I'll take Sarah. Maybe you can meet us later if things improve.''

"Kate, I'm sorry. Sarah will be so disappointed."

He was right. Her daughter had been looking forward to having all three of them—Kate, Eric and Anna—in the audience. "Like a family," she'd told Kate happily. But it couldn't be helped.

"I'll explain it to her, Eric. Don't worry."

"I wish Mom hadn't agreed to go early to help set up refreshments." She heard the frustration in his voice. "At least you could have ridden together, then."

"Please, Eric. It's okay. We're fine. Just do what you can for that poor child and his parents."

"Thanks, Kate."

"For what?"

"For understanding. For not making me feel guilty. For not hating my work and resenting the demands and the disruption."

Once again Kate had a glimpse of the hell he must have lived through with Cindy.

"Eric, your profession is part of who you are," she said quietly. "Your conscientiousness and caring are two of the things I lo—'' She paused and cleared her throat. "Things I respect in you and find appealing. So stop worrying and go do your job, okay?"

"Okay. And I'll get there as soon as I can. You'll explain to Sarah? Tell her I'm sorry?"

"Yes. Everything will be fine. We'll see you later."

"Count on it."

As Kate slowly replaced the receiver, Sarah trailed excitedly into the kitchen, holding her halo. "When do we have to leave, Mommy?"

Kate took her hand and drew her into the living room, tucking her under her arm as they sat down. "In about fifteen minutes. Honey, you know how Dr. Eric was supposed to take us?"

Sarah looked up at her with wide eyes that were suddenly troubled. "Yes."

"Well, he's at the hospital. There's a very sick little boy there who needs him very much. And his mommy and daddy are very worried and they need Dr. Eric, too. So he has to stay with them for a while and try to help that little boy get well so he can go home for Christmas."

Sarah's lower lip began to quiver. "Isn't Dr. Eric coming to see me in the Christmas pageant?"

"He's going to try his very best, honey. But he isn't sure he'll be able to get there in time. This little boy needs him. Just think if you were sick and had to go to the hospital. Wouldn't you want Dr. Eric to stay with you?"

"Yes. But he said he'd come to my show. And I need him, too."

"I know, honey. And Dr. Eric knows, too. It's just that sometimes, when you're a doctor, other people need you more. This little boy is so sick that he might die if Dr. Eric doesn't stay with him."

"You mean like Daddy?"

"Yes. Just like Daddy. And then his mommy and daddy would be all alone, just like we were after Daddy went to heaven."

"And they would be very sad, wouldn't they? Like you used to be?"

"Yes, they would."

Sarah bit her lip and struggled with that idea. "I

guess maybe they do need Dr. Eric more," she said at last in a small voice.

Kate's heart swelled, and she pulled Sarah close. "Oh, sweetie, I'm so proud of you. You're such a big girl! Why don't we say a prayer for the little boy so that God will watch over him?"

"Okay."

As they held hands on the couch and sent a heartfelt plea to the Lord, Kate also took a moment to silently give thanks—for the wonderful, caring man who had come into her life, and for a precious daughter who had shown a compassion and unselfishness beyond her years.

"Oh, my, will you look at that!"

Anna stood at the window of the church hall and gazed outside. A mixture of sleet and snow had begun to fall during the program, and the roads were already covered. Kate, who stood at her elbow, felt the color drain from her face. Eric hadn't made it to the pageant, and there was still no sign of him. The road would only get worse the longer she waited, and even though the social was just beginning, she decided to call it a night.

"I think I'm going to head home, Anna," she said, trying to control the tremor in her voice. "I'm not much for driving in bad weather."

Anna turned back to her. "Well, I can't say I blame you. But you'll have to pry Sarah away from the dessert table."

Kate glanced at her daughter, whose obvious delight in the wonderland of sweets brought a fleeting smile to Kate's face. "We'll just have to get a plate to go. How about you? Will you be okay getting home?'' she asked worriedly.

"Oh, absolutely. Fred and Jenny have a four-wheel drive. In fact, if you want to wait, you could ride with us and just leave your car here."

Kate considered the offer for a moment, then regretfully shook her head. "Thanks, Anna. I'd love to take you up on that, but I need the car for school tomorrow."

"Well, you be careful then, okay?"

"I will."

By the time Kate and Sarah were strapped into their older-model compact car, the icy mixture had intensified. Kate glanced nervously at Sarah, but fortunately she was so busy sampling her smorgasbord of desserts that she seemed oblivious to her mother's tension. Which was just as well, Kate concluded. With any luck, they'd be home before Sarah even made a dent in her plate of goodies.

Eric swung into the church parking lot, skidding slightly as he made the turn. For the first time he realized that it was sleeting. He'd been so distraught since he'd left the hospital that he hadn't even noticed the weather. He'd simply turned on the windshield defroster and made the drive to the church on automatic pilot, his mind in a turmoil.

Was there anything else he could have done? he asked himself for the dozenth time in the last hour. Had he reacted quickly enough? Had he pushed the tests through as rapidly as possible? Would it have made any difference if they'd made the diagnosis even half an hour sooner? And dear God, how did you explain to two grief-stricken parents that you'd let their only child die? They'd stared at him numbly, in shock and disbelief, and all he'd been able to say was, "I'm sorry." "Inadequate" didn't even come close to describing those words.

Eric parked the car and took a long, shaky breath. Even after years of dealing with scenarios like this, he'd never gotten used to it. Some doctors learned to insulate themselves from the pain. He never had. On nights like this it ripped through him like a knife, leaving his heart in shreds, his spirits crushed.

Wearily he climbed out of the car and made his way toward the church hall. He wasn't in the mood to see anyone, not even Kate, but he'd promised to come if he could. And he wasn't a man who gave his word lightly. So when he'd left the hospital he'd just automatically headed in this direction.

"Heavens, Eric, are you all right?"

Anna met him inside the door, her face a mask of concern.

He jammed his hands into the deep pockets of his jacket. "Not especially."

"Kate told me about your patient. Did he…"

"He didn't make it." His voice was flat and lifeless.

Anna's eyes filled with tears and she reached out to touch his arm. "Oh, Eric, I'm sorry. I know how losses like this tear you up."

"I'm in great shape compared to the parents."

"I know you did all you could," Anna said quietly.

He sighed and wearily raked the fingers of one hand through his hair. "I hope so." He glanced around the room and frowned. "Is the pageant over?"

"It's been over for twenty minutes. Would you like some coffee?"

Distractedly he shook his head, his gaze once more scanning the room. "Where's Kate? And Sarah?"

"They left about five minutes ago. Kate said she didn't want to wait in case the weather got any worse."

For the first time since leaving the hospital his mind switched gears. Kate hated to drive in this kind of weather. And now she was out there on roads that were rapidly becoming treacherous, probably as terrified as she'd been on the drive home from Tennessee. His frown deepened and he turned toward the door.

"I'll call you tomorrow, Mom," he called over his shoulder, not waiting for a reply.

As Eric set off on the familiar route from the church to Kate's apartment, his heart began to hammer against his rib cage. He drove as quickly as the deteriorating conditions would allow, peering ahead, his hands gripping the wheel. *Please, Lord, watch over her,* he prayed. *Let her feel Your presence and Your guiding hand.*

By the time he caught sight of her, she was only about a mile from her apartment. She was driving slowly and cautiously, but she was safe, he reassured himself, his shoulders sagging in relief. In a couple of minutes he'd be right behind her, and a few minutes after that, she'd be home.

Eric watched as Kate stopped at an intersection. She took plenty of time to look in both directions, then continued across. But for some reason she stopped right in the middle. Or perhaps her car stalled or got stuck on the ice. He wasn't sure. All he knew was that he suddenly saw headlights approaching too quickly, heard the squeal of brakes, and then watched in horror as the other car slammed into the passenger side of Kate's vehicle.

For the second time in a handful of hours, Eric felt as if someone had kicked him in the gut. He stepped on the accelerator, oblivious to the road conditions, and skidded to a stop with only inches to spare. The other driver was already out of his car and clearly unhurt.

"Do you have a cell phone?" Eric shouted as he slipped and slid across the icy surface. The man nodded. "Call 911," Eric barked harshly.

He didn't want to look inside Kate's car. But he had no choice. Hiding from what was inside the car was as impossible as hiding from what was in his heart.

He tried Sarah's door first, but it was too smashed to budge and he couldn't tell how seriously hurt she was by peering in the window. All he knew was that she was crying.

Eric moved around to the driver's side as quickly as the icy conditions would allow, and when he pulled open the door the wrenching sound of Sarah's sobbing spilled out. Kate was leaning across the seat, frantically trying to unbuckle her daughter's seat belt, but she was too constrained by her own. Eric reached in and unsnapped it, freeing her.

"Kate, are you all right?"

If she heard him, she didn't respond. Her attention was focused solely on her daughter.

He tried again, this time more forcefully, his hands firmly on her shoulders, a touch of desperation in his voice. "Kate, look at me. I need to know if you're all right."

She turned then, her eyes frantic. For a moment she

didn't even seem to recognize him, and when she did, her face crumpled. "Eric? Oh, God, where were you? We needed you! Please...help us! Help Sarah!"

Eric felt as if a knife had just been thrust into his heart and ruthlessly twisted. Those few words, and the look of hurt and betrayal on her face, sent his world crashing so rapidly that it left him reeling. But he couldn't think about that now. There were other, more pressing things that demanded his attention.

"Kate, are you hurt?" he repeated, his voice broken and raspy.

Jerkily she shook her head, then clutched at his arm. "No. I'm okay. Please...just help Sarah!"

"I'm going to. Can you get out? I can't get in from her side."

Kate nodded and scrambled out, swaying unsteadily as she stood. He reached for her, but she shook him off impatiently, clinging to the frigid metal of the car as the sleet stung her face. "Go to Sarah."

Eric climbed into the front seat and reached over to touch Sarah, speaking softly. "Sarah, it's Dr. Eric. I'm going to help you, okay? Sarah? Can you look at me?"

Her sobbing abated slightly and she turned to him, her eyes wide with fear. At first he thought the dark splotches on her face were blood and his stomach lurched. But then he noticed the plate of cake and cookies on the floor and realized it was chocolate. He drew a steadying breath.

"Sarah, can you tell me what hurts?"

"M-my ar-arm," she said tearfully.

"I'll tell you what. I'm going to unbuckle your seat belt and take a look, okay?" He tried to keep his voice calm and matter-of-fact, but it took every ounce of discipline he had.

"I want my mommy," Sarah declared, her lower lip beginning to tremble.

"I'm here, Sarah." Kate leaned into the car. "Do what Dr. Eric says, okay?"

She sniffled. "Okay."

"Sarah, honey, can you turn toward me? I just want to take a look at your arm. I promise I'll try not to hurt you." Eric reached over and unsnapped her seat belt as he spoke, holding it away from her body as it slid into its holder.

She angled toward him slightly, her sobs subsiding. Fortunately she was wearing a down-filled parka, he noted. It had probably padded her somewhat from the impact. But it also hampered his exam. He reached over and took her small hand in his, forcing himself to smile.

"It looks like you had chocolate cake tonight. Was it good?" he asked, gently manipulating her arm.

"Yes. But I didn't get to finish it."

"Well, we'll just have to get you some more. Maybe your very own cake."

Her eyes grew wide. "Really?"

"Really." He unzipped her parka and eased it off her shoulders. "Do you want chocolate or yellow?"

"Chocolate."

"Ah. A woman after my own heart." He carefully pressed her arm in critical places through the thin knit of her sweater, slowly working his way up. "I think that's a good choice. Chocolate or white icing?"

"Chocolate. And maybe it could have— Ouch!" She gave a startled yelp when he reached her elbow.

"I'm sorry, honey. Does it hurt up here, too?" Carefully he pressed along her upper arm to her shoulder. Silently she shook her head.

"How is everything in here, Doctor?"

Eric turned, suddenly aware of the flashing red lights reflecting off the icy pavement. A police officer was looking into the car.

"Nothing too serious, as far as I can tell."

"Should I call an ambulance?"

That would only upset Kate and Sarah even more, he decided. "I'll take them to the hospital."

"Okay. I'll send one of my men over to take a statement."

Eric nodded, then turned back to Sarah and draped the parka over her shoulders. "I don't want to hurt your arm, honey. Can you scoot over and put your other arm around my neck?"

Sarah nodded, and a moment later he eased himself out of the car, with Sarah in his arms. Kate reached out to her daughter and touched her face, then turned anxious eyes to Eric.

"I don't think there's any real damage," he said reassuringly. "But I'd like to get you both checked out at the hospital, just to be sure."

Kate shook her head. "I'm fine. I'm just worried about Sarah."

Kate didn't look fine. She looked terrible. Her face was colorless and she was visibly shaking. But he wasn't about to stand around in the sleet and argue.

"Hold on to my arm. We'll take my car."

She frowned. "What about my car? Is it drivable?"

"Yes, ma'm," the police officer replied, coming up next to them. "The keys are still in the ignition, so if you'll give us your address, we'll drop it off when we're finished here.''

Kate complied, and a few moments later they were on their way to the hospital. Though Eric tried to convince Kate to be examined, she refused.

"I told you, Eric. I'm not hurt. Just shaken up. I'll feel much better when I know for sure that Sarah is all right.''

Which she was, except for a badly bruised elbow, Eric concluded after a complete exam at the hospital. Kate's shoulders sagged with relief when he told her, and she lifted a weary, trembling hand to her forehead as tears spilled out of her eyes.

"Thank God!" she whispered fervently.

Eric wanted to reach out to Kate, wanted to take her in his arms and comfort her. Wanted to feel the comfort of *her* arms. But he held himself back. Her words at the accident scene, though spoken in a moment of panic and fear, had seared themselves into his soul, "Where were you? We needed you!" In circumstances like that, people often said what was truly in their heart. Cindy had just been more direct about it. "You're never there when I need you," had been her frequent refrain. And she had been right. Just as Kate had been right a couple of hours before. If he'd attended the pageant, as he'd promised, the accident would never have happened. They would have stayed for the social, and their paths would never have crossed with the other driver. Once again, his profession had gotten in the way of his private life—and with consequences that could have been so much worse. And it could very likely happen again. Which led Eric to the disheartening conclusion he'd reached long ago.

Marriage and medicine didn't mix.

Chapter Twelve

Something was very wrong.

Kate frowned and slowly replaced the receiver, then turned to stare out the window at the leaden skies and the barren trees cloaked in a dull, gray fog. *Everything* suddenly looked gray to her, she realized, her eyes misting with tears—including the future that so recently had seemed golden.

Ever since the accident four days ago, Eric had been like a different person. He'd brought Sarah her own miniature chocolate cake, just as he'd promised in the car on the night of the accident. He'd offered to drive Kate anywhere she needed to go, even though she had a rental car while her own was being repaired. He checked daily to see how she and Sarah were doing. In fact, she'd just hung up from his call. But in many ways she felt as if she'd been talking to a polite stranger. There was a distance between them, an almost palpable separation that made her feel cold and afraid.

At first Kate thought it was because of the little boy

he'd lost. And that probably *was* part of it, she reflected. He wasn't the kind of man who would ever be able to insulate his heart from such a tragedy. But the distance she felt was due to more than that, she was sure. For some reason the accident that had damaged her car had also damaged something far more valuable—their relationship. And she wasn't sure why. She'd tried to bring it up a couple of times, but Eric had simply said that he was busy at work, and they could talk about it after the holidays. Which did nothing to ease her mind.

Restlessly Kate rose and began to pace, her worry deepening. Eric was slipping away. She could feel it as surely as she'd felt the sting of sleet against her cheeks on the night of the accident. And she couldn't let that happen. Not without a fight, anyway. Not when she'd begun to build her whole future around this special man. But how did you fight an unknown enemy? How did you tackle a phantom, a shadow?

Kate didn't know. But suddenly she thought of someone who might.

"Kate! This is a surprise!" Amy exclaimed. "Did you change your mind and decide to come down for Christmas? You know you and Eric and Sarah are more than welcome. And you won't even have to put up with Wally this time. I'm pleased to report that our guest has thankfully been returned to his owner in good health and with good riddance, just in time for the holidays. Hallelujah!"

Kate found herself smiling despite her anxiety. "Since you did such a good job, maybe Cal's friend will ask you to iguana-sit again next year."

"Bite your tongue!" Amy declared in horror.

"Just a thought."

"And not a good one. But speaking of good thoughts, I'm serious about the invitation. Do you think you can drag that hardworking doctor down here for a quick visit?"

Kate played with the phone cord. "Frankly, I doubt I could convince him to visit anyone. Even me."

There was a moment of silence while Amy processed this information. When she spoke, her voice was laced with concern. "Do you want to tell me what happened?"

"I honestly don't know," Kate admitted, struggling to control the tears that suddenly welled in her eyes. "It's just that ever since the accident, he..."

"Whoa! Back up! What accident?" Amy demanded in alarm.

A pang of guilt ricocheted through Kate. She should have told Amy sooner, but she'd had other things on her mind—namely her relationship with Eric. "It wasn't bad, Amy. Don't worry. Some guy ran into our car the other night on the way back from the Christmas pageant. It was sleeting, and he lost control."

"Are you and Sarah all right?"

"Sarah's elbow is bruised, but it's nothing serious. I'm fine."

"How about Eric?"

Kate frowned. "What do you mean?"

"Was he hurt?"

"Oh. He wasn't in the car. He was delayed at the hospital. By the time he got to church we'd left, so he followed us. He was right behind us when the accident happened."

"You mean he saw the whole thing?"

"Yes."

"Wow! That must have played havoc with his nerves. It gives me chills just to think about it. And that's when things changed between the two of you?"

"Yes."

"Maybe he's just upset, Kate," Amy speculated. "Watching something like that unfold in front of your eyes, seeing people you care about in danger and not being able to do anything about it... It probably shook him up pretty badly."

"I know. And to make matters worse, he'd just lost a patient." Kate briefly explained about the little boy with meningitis.

"Oh, Kate!" Amy exclaimed in horror. "Having met Eric, I imagine he was devastated."

"Yes, he was."

"Okay, so let's try to piece this together," she reasoned. "He'd already had a terrible day at the hospital. Then, not only did he disappoint Sarah, who was looking forward to having him at the pageant, but he wasn't able to drive you. You told me once that his first marriage was more or less a disaster, largely because of conflicts between his career and personal life. And that for a long time he was afraid marriage and medicine didn't mix. Maybe those old fears have resurfaced. He probably figures that if he had taken you, the accident might never have happened. But his job got in the way." She paused, and when she spoke again her voice was thoughtful. "You know, I'd lay odds that right now he's waging a pretty intense battle with guilt. And fear."

As usual, Amy's analytical mind had distilled the

essence of the situation. "You might be right," Kate conceded.

"Maybe he thinks you're upset because he didn't make the pageant. Maybe he thinks you blame him for what happened."

"But that's ridiculous! It wasn't his fault!"

"Did you tell him that?"

Kate frowned. No, she hadn't. In fact, what *had* she said to him the night of the accident? The whole incident was still so fuzzy. She remembered him pulling open her door, and she recalled the immense relief she'd felt, and her silent "Thank God!" But she hadn't said that. Nor had she said, "I'm so glad you're here," though she'd thought that, as well. She struggled to remember her first words to him, and was almost sorry when she did, for her heart sank.

"Oh, no! I couldn't have..." she whispered bleakly, closing her eyes, wishing with every ounce of her being that she could take back those accusatory words, spoken without thinking, in a moment of panic.

"Kate? What is it?"

"I just remembered what I said when Eric arrived on the accident scene," she said in dismay.

"What?"

Kate drew a deep breath. "Basically, I implied that he wasn't there for us when we needed him. Which of course only played right into the guilt he was already feeling. Big time. Oh, Amy, what am I going to do? I didn't mean it the way it came out! I was just so frightened and worried about Sarah. I don't even know where those words came from. He must have felt like he was reliving a nightmare. Just when he was starting to believe that marriage and medicine *could* mix, I say something stupid like that and blow the whole thing. He had enough guilt laid on him in his first marriage to last a lifetime. He's sure not going to put himself in that position again. No wonder he backed off!''

"You do have a problem," Amy conceded soberly. "Up until that point, do you think things were getting pretty...serious?"

"Very. In fact, I think he was..." She swallowed past the lump in her throat. "I think he was going to ask me to marry him, Amy."

"Were you going to accept?"

"Yes."

"Then you can't let this setback stand in the way," she declared resolutely.

"But I can't take back those words. And he isn't likely to forget them."

"I agree. What you need now are some more words."

"Do you want to explain that?"

"Let me ask you something first, Kate. How much do you love Eric?"

"So much that I can't even imagine a future without him anymore," she replied softly, without hesitation.

"Then you love him enough to do something totally out of character?"

"What exactly do you have in mind?" Kate asked, suddenly cautious.

"Just answer the question."

Kate drew a deep breath. She wasn't sure she was going to be comfortable with whatever Amy was going to suggest. But she also knew that her sister's advice would be sound. It always was. "Yes."

"Good," Amy declared with satisfaction. "Because I have a plan."

Eric frowned as he pulled up in front of his mother's house. Why was Kate's car here? He and Anna were supposed to pick up Kate and Sarah later, in time for Christmas Eve services, and they were all going to spend the day together tomorrow. Kate had canceled her usual holiday trip to Amy's when they'd made those arrangements. If she hadn't, he would have begged off from the whole thing. It was bound to be awkward.

Eric knew that Kate was confused and troubled by the change in their relationship. The intimacy they'd begun to create had been replaced by polite formality, the closeness by distance. In fact, if Christmas hadn't been only days away, he'd have cut the ties entirely by now, as painful as that would be. God knew, it wasn't what he wanted to do. But he felt he had no choice. During the last few weeks he'd gradually begun to believe that with Kate, things could be different; that she wouldn't come to resent the demands of his profession—and ultimately him—as Cindy had. And yet, in a moment of crisis, at a time when the heart often spoke truths even *it* hadn't recognized, she'd voiced a resentment, a blame, that had pierced him to his very core. He doubted whether she even recalled what she'd said. But though *she* might not remember her words, they were ones *he* could never forget.

Eric closed his eyes and gripped the steering wheel as his gut twisted painfully. With all his heart he wished there was a way out of this dilemma, an answer to the same question that had plagued him during his marriage to Cindy: where did his first loyalty lie? It was a conflict he'd never been able to reconcile. Cindy had made her opinion clear. And—intentionally or not—so had Kate. He desperately wished he could promise her it would never happen again, but that would be a lie. It *would* happen again. And again. And again. Until finally she, too, grew disillusioned and bitter. He couldn't do that to her. Or to himself.

Wearily Eric climbed out of the car. For everyone's sake he needed to be upbeat for the holiday. There would be time for sadness, for dealing with the loss of a dream, later. But getting through the next thirty-six hours with even a semblance of holiday cheer wasn't going to be easy.

The fragrant smell of pine mingling with the aroma of freshly baked cookies greeted him as he stepped inside the door, and he paused for a moment to let the warm, comforting holiday smells work their soothing magic. They took him back many years, to the happy days of his boyhood, and his lips curved up at the pleasant memories. If only life could be as simple as it had been in those idyllic days of youth, when the most pressing question he faced was whether there would be a shiny red bike under the tree, come Christmas morning.

"Eric! I thought I heard you," Anna greeted him with a smile as she stepped into the small foyer.

"Hello, Mom." He bent and kissed her cheek. "Merry Christmas."

"Merry Christmas to you. I'm glad you came early."

"You asked me to."

"So I did. It's nice to see you still listen to your mother once in a while," she teased.

"You know I'm always at your beck and call. But I'm surprised to see that Kate and Sarah are here," he remarked, striving for a casual tone. "I thought we were picking them up for services later."

"Well, when Kate called earlier, she sounded awfully lonesome. She and Sarah were all by themselves, so I invited them to come over early. I figured, why not spend the time together? I baked a ham, and there's plenty for two more. I didn't think you'd mind," she teased.

Eric hadn't said anything to his mother about his plans to stop seeing Kate, and tonight wasn't the time to break the news—not when he knew she had hopes for a wedding in the not-too-distant future. It would ruin her Christmas. And one ruined Christmas was enough. "Of course not."

"Hi, Dr. Eric!" Sarah dashed into the hallway and launched herself at him.

He reached down and swept her up. "Hi, yourself, sweetie. How's that elbow?"

She cocked it for him to see. "It's still kind of blue." Then she put her small arms around his neck and smiled. "You know what?"

His throat tightened. This was something else he was going to miss—the trusting touch of a child who loved him. "What?"

"This is the best Christmas ever!"

Eric's gut clenched again. How he hated to hurt this child! He was sure Kate would find a way to explain their breakup without making him sound like a villain. That was her way. But he sure *felt* like one. And as he looked into Sarah's happy, guileless face, so filled with the optimism of youth, he suddenly felt old.

"Sarah, honey, are you ready to decorate that next batch of cookies?" Anna asked.

"Yes. Do you want a cookie, Dr. Eric? Aunt Anna made them, and I decorated them," she told him proudly.

"I'll have one a little later," he promised as he set her down. He glanced at his mother as Sarah scampered back to the kitchen. "Where's Kate?"

"Right here," she replied breathlessly, coming up behind Anna.

As always, Eric was moved by the translucent beauty of her face. These last few weeks it had seemed almost luminous, filled with a soft light and a peace that reflected a soul at rest. But today she seemed a bit...different. He couldn't quite put his finger on it. Her eyes were a little too bright, for one thing. And her face was flushed. There was also an unusual energy radiating from her, making her movements seem agitated. He frowned, both curious and concerned.

"Are you all right?" he asked.

Her flush deepened. "Yes, of course. A little warm from all that cookie baking, though. Anna, I think I'll take a walk. I love this crisp weather, and I feel a touch of snow in the air. I won't be gone long," she promised, opening the hall closet to retrieve her coat.

"Kate, dear, do you think you should?" Anna asked worriedly. "It's getting dark."

"I'll be fine. A little fresh air will do me good."

Anna turned to Eric with a frown. "I'm not crazy about her walking alone, even if it is Christmas Eve."

"Please don't worry, Anna. I won't be gone long.

Just down to the park and back,'' Kate reassured her as she pulled on her gloves.

Eric wasn't crazy about the idea, either. But Kate seemed determined to go. He frowned, waging an internal debate. Spending time alone with her was the last thing he wanted to do. The temptation to touch her, to feel her melt into his arms, was hard enough to resist when there were other people present. He wasn't sure his self-control would hold when it was just the two of them. Despite recent events and his subsequent resolve to end their relationship, he still loved her. He still wanted her to be his wife. And deep in his heart, he still wanted to believe they could work out the conflict between their personal life as a couple and his career. But his confidence had been badly shaken. He just couldn't find the courage to trust his heart—or his judgment. They had betrayed him once. How could he be sure they wouldn't again?

"Eric, I really don't like this," Anna prompted more forcefully.

His gaze swung from Kate to Anna's concerned face, then back to Kate. He didn't, either. It wasn't safe for Kate to be wandering around in the dark by herself. There was really no choice.

"Why don't I go with you?" he suggested. "If you don't mind the company."

Did her smile seem relieved? Or was it just his imagination?

"I don't mind in the least. Thank you." She picked up a tote bag, slung it over her shoulder and gazed expectantly at Eric.

He hesitated for a moment, then pulled open the door and stepped aside. "We won't be long, Mom," he said as Kate moved past him, leaving a faint, pleasing fragrance in her wake.

"Don't hurry. We won't eat for at least an hour," she assured them.

Kate waited while he shut the door, then fell into step beside him as they headed down the sidewalk. Dusk was just beginning to fall, and the lights from Christmas trees twinkled merrily in the windows. Few cars passed, leaving the peace and stillness of the evening largely undisturbed.

"I've always liked Christmas Eve," Kate said softly. "I remember as a child it was filled with such a sense of wonder and hope and anticipation. As if great, exciting things were about to happen. Was it like that for you?"

Eric shoved his hands into the pockets of his overcoat. His breath made frosty clouds in the cold air, but his heart was warm as he thought of Christmases past. "Yes, it was. Thanks to Mom and Dad. They made me feel that somehow anything was possible during this magical season. It's a shame we have to grow up and lose that belief in endless possibilities."

They strolled for a few minutes in silence, and just as they reached the park a few large, feathery flakes began to drift down. The distant strains of "Silent Night" floated through the quiet air as carolers raised their voices in the familiar, beloved melody.

"My favorite Christmas song," Kate murmured, her lips curving up sweetly. "Could we sit for a minute?" She nodded toward a park bench tucked between two fir trees bedecked with twinkling white lights.

Eric hesitated. He was already pushing his luck, going on this walk. He'd had to fight the impulse to reach over and take her hand every step of the way. Sitting on a park bench, where the shimmering lights were sure to add a luster to her ebony hair and bring out the sparkle in her eyes, was downright dangerous. "It's getting awfully dark, Kate," he objected.

"Please, Eric? We don't have to stay long. But the song is so beautiful."

There was no way he could refuse her when she looked at him like that, her eyes soft and hopeful, her face glowing. He drew a deep breath and slowly let it out. "Okay."

Kate led the way to the bench and sat down, carefully setting the tote bag beside her. He joined her more slowly, keeping a modest distance between them. As they sat there quietly, listening to the distant, melodic voices, Eric stole a glance at Kate. She seemed oblivious to the snowflakes that clung to her hair like gossamer stars, giving her an ethereal beauty. Her gaze was fixed on something in the distance, and he wondered what she was thinking.

Please, Lord, give me the courage to go through with this, Kate prayed silently. *I've never been the bold type, but I think Amy's right. This may be the only way to convince Eric how much I care. Please, let me feel Your presence and help me to find the right words.*

As the last strains of "Silent Night" faded away, her heart began to hammer painfully against her rib cage. So before her courage could waver, she clasped her hands tightly in her lap, took a deep breath and turned to him.

"Eric, I've been thinking a lot about what happened the night of the accident. And I think we need to talk about it," she said as firmly as she could manage, considering her insides were quivering like the proverbial bowlful of jelly.

Startled, he jerked his gaze to hers. Confrontation wasn't her style, yet there was a touch of that in both her voice and the determined tilt of her chin. And she was right, of course. They did need to talk. But he didn't want to do it on Christmas Eve. "Kate, can't we put this on hold until after…"

"No." Her tone was quiet but resolved. "My life has been on hold too long, Eric." She reached into the tote bag at her feet, withdrew a flat, rectangular package and held it out to him. "Let's start with this."

He stared at the gift wrapped in silver paper. "Kate, I…"

"Please, Eric. Unlike Amy, I'm not really good at this assertiveness thing, so just humor me, okay?"

The pleading tone in her voice, the strain around its edges, tugged at his heart, and without another word he took the package and tore off the wrapping. He angled the counted-cross-stitch sampler toward the light from the bushes as he slowly read the words from Jeremiah that had been so carefully and elaborately stitched around a motif of the rising sun. "For I know well the plans I have in mind for you, says the Lord, plans for your welfare not for woe! Plans to give you a future full of hope."

"I started working on this when Jack was in the hospital," Kate told him quietly, her gaze resting on the sampler. "I came across the passage one night when I was idly leafing through the Bible, and it seemed to speak directly to my soul. Because after the accident I felt that there must have been something I did—something wrong—to deserve such a tragedy and loss. Taking Jack away was the Lord's way of punishing me, I thought. So whenever I started to feel overwhelmed, I'd pull this out and work on it to remind me that the Lord was *for* me, not *against* me. And it also encouraged me to look to the future with faith and hope. It made me believe that things would get better, that tomorrow my life would again be filled with joy."

Kate paused and transferred her gaze from the gift to his deep blue eyes. "When Jack died, I put the sampler away. I felt empty and hollow inside, and the words seemed to mock me rather than offer comfort. For a long time I lived in an emotional and spiritual vacuum. The guilt became all-consuming again, and I lost hope that the kind of love I shared with Jack, which had made my world so bright, would ever touch my life again. All I could see in my future was an endless string of dark days. And then you came along."

She drew a steadying breath, willing her courage to hold fast. "Eric, the simple fact is that until I met you, my life was like this sampler—on hold and unfinished. But you made me realize that it was time to tie up the loose threads and move on. So I did exactly that— literally and figuratively. Because when I took this out of storage, I took out my heart, as well. For the first time in five years, I let myself not only believe again in the endless possibilities of life, but I opened myself to them. I want you to have this because I think you've been held captive by the same demons that plagued me for years—guilt and hopelessness. And I think it's time for you to do what I did—put your past to rest so you can create a new future."

She paused and reached into her bag again, this time withdrawing a smaller, square box, which she handed to him. She noticed that her hands were trembling, and clasped them tightly in her lap as Eric silently unwrapped the second package, then lifted the lid. Nestled on a bed of tissue lay a delicate, heart-shaped blown-glass Christmas-tree ornament with a loop of green satin ribbon at the top, anchored with sprigs of holly.

"Just as today we celebrate the birth of a baby who brought new life to the world two thousand years ago, I'd like us to celebrate our own rebirth of hope and faith that this day symbolizes," Kate said softly. "When Jack died, I never thought I'd love again. But the Lord seemed to have other ideas when he sent you my way. Because how could I help but fall in love with your tenderness and caring and sense of humor and those deep blue eyes and all of the thousands of things that make you so very special and unique? I love you, Eric Carlson, and I can't imagine my future without you in it. So I give you this ornament as a sign of what you've already claimed—my heart. And I would be very honored if...if you would marry me."

Eric stared at her, speechless, then looked down at the shiny red ornament cradled in his hands. It was so fragile and so easily broken—just like her heart. Dear God, had she really offered to entrust it to his care? Or was he caught up in some sort of Christmas Eve fantasy? His confused gaze moved to her hands, clasped tightly in her lap, and he could sense the tension vibrating in every nerve of her body as she waited for his reaction. So it was real, after all.

A rush of tenderness and love and elation swept over him, so swift and powerful that it took his breath away—and scared him out of his wits. There was no question that he returned her love, with every ounce of his being. Yet doubts about making a success of marriage, given the pressures of his career, remained. He struggled against the urge to throw caution to the wind and pull her into his arms and shout "Yes!" for all the world to hear. It was what his heart told him to do. But he had to make sure she understood the dangers.

"Kate, I—" His voice broke and he cleared his throat.

Kate felt the bottom drop out of her stomach. She'd obviously shocked him into speechlessness, and her courage suddenly deserted her. How could she possibly have asked this man to marry her? Amy's bold plan had seemed reasonable when they'd discussed it, but given his reaction, it was way off base. Now she needed to find a way to smooth over the awkwardness she'd created.

"Listen, Eric, I'm sorry," she said jerkily. "Y-you don't have to answer that question. I understand if…"

He reached out and took her hand, his look so tender and warm that her voice deserted her. "I *want* to answer the question. I was just…overwhelmed for a minute. No one's ever proposed to me before." His lips quirked into a crooked grin.

Although the ardent light in his eyes set her heart hammering, she sensed a hesitation in his manner. She had hoped her bold question would assuage any doubts he might have about her willingness to accept the demands his job would make on their life, but apparently it hadn't, she realized with dismay.

"I—I understand if you need to think about it," she stammered, stalling for time, suddenly afraid to hear his answer. If he was going to refuse, she didn't want to know tonight. Not on Christmas Eve. She averted her gaze and reached for the tote bag. "Like you said, we can talk about this after Christmas."

She started to stand, but he restrained her and pulled her trembling body close beside him, into the shelter of his arm. "You can't just drop something like that on a man and then walk away, you know. Let's talk."

She lowered her head and stared at the snowflakes falling gently to the ground, willing the peace of that sight to calm the turbulence in her heart. "I don't know what else to say," she responded softly, her voice choked with emotion.

Eric reached over and with gentle pressure urged her chin back up until their gazes met. "Then I'll start. First of all, I love you, too," he said huskily.

Kate's throat constricted, and joy flooded her heart. Those were the words she'd been praying to hear for weeks! And yet…he hadn't accepted her proposal. She searched his eyes, afraid to ask but knowing she had to. "I sense a 'but' there," she ventured, her voice quavering.

He laced his fingers with hers and absently stroked his thumb across the back of her hand.

"There is," he conceded. "I'm just not sure marriage would be good for either of us."

"How can you say that, when we love each other?"

"Because love implies certain obligations. Like being there for a child's Christmas play. And making sure the woman you love doesn't have to deal with her private terrors alone. And protecting the people you love from danger. And honoring promises. And a million other things that my profession won't always allow me to do. What happened four days ago could happen again, Kate. I can't promise you it won't."

"I'm not asking you to. I admire your dedication to your work, Eric. It's part of what makes you who you are. Don't you think I know that you're torn between what you see as conflicting loyalties, that you anguish over balancing the two responsibilities? I wish you wouldn't let it tear you up inside. Yet one of the reasons I love you is that you care enough to *feel* anguish. And my feelings about *that* will never change."

He wanted to believe her. Desperately. But experience had been a harsh teacher. "I'd like to think that's true, Kate," he said wearily. "And I know you believe it is—right now. But I'm afraid that in time you'll come to resent my work. Whether you realize it or not, you were upset the night of the accident because I wasn't there for you."

"You're thinking about that stupid comment I made when you opened my door, aren't you?" she said quietly.

He looked surprised. "You remember what you said?"

"Yes. And obviously you do, too. Eric, I don't know where those words came from. I was distraught. And shaken up. And afraid Sarah was hurt. I wasn't even thinking straight. Do you know what my *thoughts* were when you appeared? 'Thank God.' I can't even find the words to describe the relief I felt when I saw you. I know my words didn't reflect that. But that was what was in my heart." She paused and took a deep breath. "Believe it or not, Eric, I can handle the fact that you have a demanding career that sometimes requires you to make difficult choices. I may be disappointed sometimes if your duties take you away from us, but I'll never stop loving you. Because I know you'll always do your best to *give* your best. To us *and* your job. I would never ask for any more than that. And I truly believe that if we trust in the Lord, He'll show us the way to make this work.''

Eric gazed into the face that had become so precious and dear to him during these last few months. The sincerity in her eyes, and the love, were unquestionable. What had he ever done to deserve a woman with such an understanding heart, and an inner beauty that surpassed even her physical loveliness? he wondered, his throat tightening with emotion. She seemed so sure, so confident about their future. Why couldn't he put his own doubts and fears to rest, as well?

"You seem to have such faith," he said quietly.

She looked at him steadily. "Enough to move mountains. I'm not Cindy, Eric. I love you for who you are—not in *spite* of who you are. And on this Christmas Eve, for the first time in years, I believe great, exciting things are about to happen. I believe that anything is possible. And I believe in you. And us."

Eric looked at her, his heart so full of love that for a moment he couldn't speak. She was everything he'd always wanted, and he suddenly knew with absolute certainty that he'd be a fool to pass up this chance for happiness. As if to confirm his sudden lightness of heart, the distant voices of the carolers came once more through the air, jubilantly proclaiming, "Joy to the World." As he reached over and touched her face with infinite tenderness, his doubt was replaced by a gladness and peace that truly reflected this most joyous, holy season.

"When I got to Mom's tonight, Sarah said that this was the best Christmas ever," Eric told Kate huskily. "And you know something? She's absolutely right."

Kate studied him cautiously, trying not to infer too much from his tender tone of voice and the promise in his eyes. Yet she was unable to stop her hopes from soaring. "Is that a yes?" she ventured.

He chuckled as his own spirits suddenly took wing. "That is most definitely a yes. And even though this proposal wasn't exactly traditional, I think we should seal it in the traditional way. Don't you agree?"

The sudden flame of passion in his eyes made her tingle. "Most definitely, " she concurred.

He reached for her, and she went willingly, savoring the haven of his strong arms and the wondrous feeling of homecoming. And in the moment before his lips claimed hers, the words of the distant carol echoed in her ears, making her heart rejoice.

"Let heaven and nature sing. Let heaven and nature sing. Let heaven, and heaven, and nature sing."

Amen, she said silently. *And thank you.*

Epilogue

Five months later

It was a perfect day for a wedding.

Kate gazed out the window of Amy's log cabin at the blue-hazed mountains, fresh with spring. New green shoots decorated the tips of the spruce trees, and the masses of rhododendrons and mountain laurel on the hillsides were heavy with pink-hued blossoms. A cloud of yellow swallowtail butterflies drifted by, undulating playfully in the warm morning sun, while classical flute music played a duet with the splashing water from a nearby stream.

Kate smiled and slowly drew in a deep breath. The peaceful setting, reflecting the beauty of God's creation and the rebirth of nature after a long, cold winter, seemed symbolic; within a few moments, she and Eric would start a new life together after their own long, cold winter of the heart.

"You look happy."

Kate turned at the sound of Amy's voice. Her sister stood in the doorway with Sarah, holding two bouquets of mountain laurel still beaded with silver drops of dew.

"I am."

"And beautiful."

Kate flushed and turned to look in the full-length mirror beside her. The simple but elegant style of her A-line, tea-length gown enhanced her slender figure, and the overlay of delicate chiffon that flared out near the hem softly swirled as she moved. Long sleeves—sheer and full, cuffed at the wrist—emphasized her delicate bone structure, and the deep blue color was a perfect foil for her dark hair and flawless complexion.

"I *feel* beautiful," she admitted. And young. And breathless. And hopeful. And all the things every bride should feel on her special day, she thought with wonder.

"Do I look pretty, too, Mommy?" Sarah asked.

Kate turned to her daughter and smiled. In her white eyelet dress, with a basket of flowers in her hands, she would fit right in at a Victorian garden party.

"You look lovely," Kate replied, kneeling down to hold her close. Without Sarah, she knew she would never have survived the months following Jack's death. Only her daughter's sunny disposition and innocent laughter had kept her sane and grounded in the present, prevented her from slipping into the abyss of total despair. She hugged Sarah fiercely, thanking God for His gift of the precious child who had filled her life with a special love during the difficult years when she'd felt so deserted and spiritually alone.

When Kate finally released her, Sarah lifted her basket and pointed to a bluebell. "I picked that flower for Dr. Eric. Aunt Amy says I can give it to him later."

Kate smiled, deeply grateful that Sarah adored Eric. And equally grateful that the feeling was returned.

"I'm sure he'll like that. It's just the color of his eyes."

"Well, if you two ladies are ready, I don't think we should keep the groom waiting any longer," Amy announced.

Kate gave Sarah one more quick hug. "I love you, honey," she whispered.

"I love you, too, Mommy."

Kate rose and Amy handed her one of the bouquets. For a long moment their gazes met and held.

"You know how happy I am for you, don't you?" Amy said softly.

Kate nodded, and when she spoke her voice was choked with tears. "I know. And thank you, Amy. For everything. For your love and support and for always being there. You and Mom were my lifeline for so many years."

Amy's own voice was none too steady when she replied, "I always will be, Kate. But I'm more than happy to share the job with someone else. Especially Eric."

The flute music suddenly changed, and Kate recognized the melody of the hymn they'd chosen for the opening of the ceremony.

"It's time," Amy said.

Kate nodded. Amy took Sarah's hand and they preceded Kate down the steps and out the door. She waited for a few moments, then stepped out into the sunshine and walked slowly toward the gazebo banked by blossoming rhododendrons and surrounded by the people she loved most in the world.

Anna was there, of course, beaming with joy. Cal smiled at her and winked, juggling Caitlin in one arm while the twins clung to his leg and stared wide-eyed at the proceedings. Frank grinned and gave a subtle thumbs-up signal.

And Eric—her breath caught in her throat as she gazed at him. He looked incredibly handsome in a dove-gray suit that hugged his broad shoulders. The morning sun had turned his blond hair to gold, and as she gazed into his face—so fine and strong and compassionate and caring—tears of happiness pricked her eyes. His own eyes, so blue and tender, caught and held hers compellingly as she drew closer. They spoke more eloquently than words of the passion and love and commitment in his heart, and she trembled with wonder that God had blessed her with a second chance at love.

As the pure notes of "Amazing Grace" drifted through the mountain air, she was glad once again that they'd chosen this hymn to begin their wedding ceremony. For she had, indeed, once been lost. But now she was found. And today, as she prepared to start a new life with the man she loved, she felt filled with God's amazing grace.

Eric watched Kate approach, and his own heart overflowed with joy. The significance of the song wasn't lost on him, either. He knew that without the Lord's help, he wouldn't be standing here today. On his own, he would never have had the courage to take another chance on love. But God had sent him Kate, whose sweetness and understanding had broken through the barriers he'd erected around his heart and made him believe once again in endless possibilities. And as Kate stepped up into the gazebo and took his hand, her eyes shining with love and faith and trust, he knew beyond the shadow of a doubt that they would have a rich, full marriage. For the Lord would always help them, just as His grace had led their hearts home.

* * * * *

Dear Reader,

As I write this, the rustle of autumn is underfoot.
Winter—that season of rest and renewal for a
slumbering world—will soon be upon us. But
like the beautiful scarlet cardinals twittering in the
tree beside my bench, and the gloriously blooming
impatiens oblivious to the inevitable frost that will
soon make them only a memory, I am reluctant to let
the warm weather go.

Yet sometimes letting go is the only way to move
forward. For without winter, we would never
appreciate the joys and promise of spring. And without
saying goodbye to the past, we can never say hello to
the future. Eric and Kate discovered that in this book.
And they also discovered that life is filled with endless
possibilities if we open our eyes—and hearts—to them.

This upcoming Christmas season, may each of you
experience the joy that comes from believing in the
endless possibilities that keep life always new.

Irene Hannon

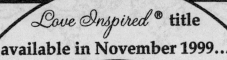

Steeple Hill's *Love Inspired*®
Title Available in November 1999...

AN ANGEL FOR DRY CREEK
by
Janet Tronstad

Glory Beckett, a police sketch artist in Seattle, witnesses a murder and is forced to flee. She finds a seemingly safe refuge in Dry Creek, Montana, at the home of Matthew Curtis and his twins. Glory helps Matthew open his heart to love again and develops a tight bond with the boys, who view her as their real-life angel. Can this "angel" face the danger of the past and protect their love?

Watch for this title in November 1999.

Available at your favorite retail outlet.

Love Inspired®

PLIAAFDC